LOVE AT THE INN

Wilkins Harbor Book 1

EMORIE COLE

Emorie Cole

Keweenaw Publishing LLC

Published in the United States by Keweenaw Publishing LLC.

Paperback ISBN 978-1-954271-01-2

FIRST EDITION

❀ Created with Vellum

Chapter One

GABBY

*I*t's a beautiful, sunny morning as I pull up in front of my new house in the Keweenaw Peninsula. My SUV is loaded down with my belongings—everything I own shoved into plastic containers and cardboard boxes. I breathe a sigh of relief as the reality finally sinks in that I'm safe, and my new life is about to begin right here in this tiny town.

As I step out of the car, I feel the cool spring air on my bare arms and shiver. I'm not used to such cold temperatures—this time of year in Arizona it still reaches at least eighty degrees. Here in Wilkins Harbor, Michigan, it's only in the forties. With it being late spring—only a couple of weeks away from summer—I expected the temperatures to be a bit warmer, but there are still small patches of snow on the ground.

I walk up the short walkway to the front door to meet my real estate agent, Samantha, who is waiting for me on the veranda with the keys. "Welcome to Wilkins Harbor, Gabby," she says with a smile. "How was the drive?"

"Long," I say tiredly. "Very long. Thanks so much for arranging my early move-in."

"No problem. The seller was more than happy to hand over the keys a few days early when I explained your situation. You just need to come to my office on Monday to finalize the paperwork."

"I'll be there bright and early on Monday morning to sign the paperwork," I reassure her.

Samantha hands over the keys and says, "It's all yours. Take a look."

Usually people buying a home *see* it first, but I didn't have the luxury of viewing it before putting in my offer. My friend Alyssa sent me a listing for this cute little blue bungalow, and offered to meet with a realtor to check it out for me when she found out that I was planning on moving to escape from my ex-boyfriend, Tim. Tim had gotten involved with a new group of friends and whenever he was around them he became angry and violent towards me and others.

I no longer felt safe being with him, or even around him for that matter.

Alyssa had met with Samantha to view the house, and we did a video call while they walked through it. It wasn't ideal, but I was at least able to get a feel for the house, and see that there was nothing major wrong with it. I had made an offer on the house immediately, having already saved up money over the last couple of years.

Holding the keys in my hand, I hesitate. "I know it's unusual to close on a home in less than thirty days —I originally planned on moving at the end of the month—so could you please let the seller know that I really appreciate her working with me?" I ask.

"Of course. She was more than happy to accommodate you when I told her what you were going through." The look on my face must be one of panic because Samantha quickly adds, "Don't worry. I only told her the basics. It's not my story to tell. That's your choice if you want to divulge all of the details or not."

"Thank you. I'm not sure I'm quite ready to share that my ex and his new group of friends, who happen to be criminals, planned on robbing a bank, and threatened me when I overheard their conversation. You're the only person I've told—I haven't even shared the exact reason with Alyssa yet, she only knows that I was moving to get away—but I figured when I called you to see if I could get the keys early, I needed to fill you in completely."

"Well, thank you for trusting me with the information." Samantha hesitates for a moment, leaning against the rail of the veranda, before asking, "It's really none of my business, but—did you report what you heard?"

"Yes, I did. As soon as I hung up the phone with you, I packed all of my belongings and hid them. When Tim left for work the next morning I packed everything into my SUV, and drove straight to the police department. They had me file a report on the information I overheard, and a second report on Tim threatening to kill me if I didn't keep my mouth shut. Obviously they needed to open an investigation first, and hopefully they stopped the robbery, but I agreed to return if they need me to testify in person. That scares the hell out of me, though."

Samantha shivers. "Wow. I can't even imagine how terrifying all of that must have been."

"The last couple of days have definitely been rough, but now I feel like I can relax. At least a little."

"Have you talked to Alyssa at all?"

"Yeah, I called her on my way here to let her know that I'd be arriving in Michigan sooner than planned. I just told her I would fill her in on the rest of the details later."

"Good. Okay, enough about that. Go check out your new home."

"Okay, I'm ready." Turning the key in the lock, I push the door open slowly. I take a deep breath as I step inside, and look to see what this new chapter of my life will be like. I feel anxious, nervous, and excited all at the same time. But I know, deep in my heart, that I'll be okay.

I smile from ear to ear as I take in the sight of my new bungalow. It's just as adorable in person as it was in my video call with Alyssa. The living room has a beautiful stone-surrounded fireplace, with light grey stones reaching from the floor to the ceiling. The room is open concept, flowing directly into the small kitchen that has a granite countertop with a decent amount of workspace. All of the appliances stand out with their stainless steel against the deep mahogany colored cabinets. The hardwood floors throughout most of the house are the same rich color as the cabinets. Soft grey carpet lines the floors in the main bedroom and the small guest bedroom. The one bathroom has a small vanity counter next to the sink, and a porcelain tub with shower. "Wow, it's beautiful, Samantha. I love it!" I say excitedly as I walk back into the living room and admire the view from the window.

"I'm so glad you do. It really is a wonderful little house. And as you can see from that window, you have a pretty good view of Lake Superior."

"It's gorgeous! I'm going to love gazing out at the boats that come through here in the summertime— Alyssa told me all about them. She said that the docks are usually busy with the sightseeing cruises and the occasional tourist yachts that dock here for a couple of weeks."

Samantha smiles. "I highly recommend you take one of the sunset cruises. Watching the sun go down over the water is breathtaking. Plus, cruising past the Edwards Mansion when it's all lit up at night is quite a sight."

"The Edwards Mansion?" I ask curiously.

"The Edwards Mansion is an elegant old mansion owned by the Edwards family. It used to be their family home, passed on to each generation, but about fifty years ago William and Elizabeth Edwards decided to turn it into a family-run inn. They retired a couple of years ago, so now it's run by their grandson, Brandon."

"Wow, that definitely sounds like something I need to see."

"The outside grounds are open to the public, not

just guests, so you are welcome to explore them if you'd like."

"Thanks for telling me. I might do that once I finish unpacking."

Samantha looks around a bit nervously. "About that—I know that you only have your vehicle packed with boxes since you had to leave so suddenly. You weren't able to arrange to bring any of your furniture, were you?"

"No. Unfortunately I was only able to bring what I could fit in my SUV. I didn't have time to arrange anything for my furniture—and I'm not sure I would want to anyway. Tim and I had bought everything together."

"Oh—I'm so sorry to hear that," she says sympathetically.

"It's alright. I have a sleeping bag and pillow to sleep on the floor for now—and the carpet looks comfy enough. I'll go furniture shopping this weekend."

"I know we've just met, but if you need any help I'd be more than happy to let you borrow some of the staging pieces I have in storage until you find something," Samantha offers kindly.

"No, it's alright. Really. My parents gave me some extra money to help out. They just wanted me as far away from Tim as possible—and as fast as possible. But thank you for offering."

"Of course. You'll find that our small community will do anything to help out a neighbor in need," she smiles. "I'll get out of your way so you can get settled. Just let me know if you need anything, and I'll see you bright and early on Monday morning."

"Thanks again for everything. See you Monday." I close the door behind her and lean back against it, glancing once again around my new house. I'm finally here and I feel like I can breathe easy for the first time in a long time. There's no need to keep looking over my shoulder to see if I'm being followed by one of Tim's *friends*. No need to hide from Tim's angry glances every time I come home while he has people over. No need to constantly worry about overhearing something that will get me killed. I can finally just relax, and move on with my life.

Stepping away from the door, I walk over to my purse, where I had placed it earlier on the kitchen counter, to grab my cell phone. After sending a quick text message to my parents to let them know that I've arrived safely, I call Alyssa.

"Hey, Gabby!" she says happily as she answers. "Where are you?"

"I'm here in Wilkins Harbor, I'm at my new house."

"I'm so happy you made it here safely! It'll be great living near each other again where we can hang out on a regular basis."

"You mean have weekly movie nights like we did when we were college roommates?" I say with a laugh.

"Exactly! So how do you like the house?"

"I *love* it! It's perfect! Thank you so much for helping me find it. I feel like I can finally be safe again."

"Of course. What are friends for?"

"So, I need to unpack my SUV first, but then do you want to go for lunch? Show me around the town a bit, maybe help me pick out some furniture?"

"Definitely! Do you need any help unpacking? I can come over and help if you want."

"Sure, that would be great. Thanks."

"Okay, I'll see you soon, Gabby."

"See you soon," I say as I end the call.

While I wait for Alyssa to arrive, I start unpacking by grabbing the small overnight bag that is packed with a few days worth of clothes. Digging around in the bag, I find the *one* long sleeve shirt that managed to get tossed into the bag instead of a box. After pulling the shirt on over my head, I bring the bag into the master bedroom and set it down against the wall before going back outside to unload a few more items.

As I'm making my third trip into the house, I see Alyssa pull into the driveway. I quickly set the box that I'm carrying down in the living room and head back outside to greet her. "Hey!" I say as I give her a hug. "It's been a while since I saw you last."

"I know. It's been way too long. Now let's get these boxes unpacked. We have a lot of time to catch up for."

"You bet we do." I let out a chuckle, and grab a box from my SUV.

Alyssa grabs a plastic bin, and follows me into the house. "This shouldn't take too long with the two of us. Plus, I'll get my workout in for the day," she says with a grin.

We carry boxes and plastic bins into the house until my SUV is finally empty. "Done. Finally," I say carrying the last of the boxes inside. "Thanks for helping. I feel like I would have been here all day otherwise."

"No problem. Are you ready for lunch?"

"Yes! I'm starving!"

"Me too," Alyssa says. "I know the perfect place to go, and it's right on the water. Come on, I'll drive."

I toss my phone into my purse, grab my house keys, and the two of us head out to Alyssa's car, locking the door behind us. On the way to the restaurant Alyssa points out several of her favorite places, including an ice cream shop and the movie theater. "Once you're all settled, we'll have to have our first movie night!" Alyssa says excitedly.

"Of course!" I say as we pull into the parking lot of the restaurant. "But first I need food and furniture —in *that* order—and then I want to check out someplace my realtor, Samantha, mentioned."

"Oh yeah? What place is that?" Alyssa asks as we make our way inside.

"Edwards Mansion. Have you ever been there?"

"Ah, yes. Edwards Mansion. Yeah, I've been there. Some of my family members stayed there when they came to visit me last summer. The inn is *gorgeous*!"

"That's what Samantha said."

We walk up to the maître d' stand and are greeted by a tall, dark-haired man. "Hi, my name is Eric. Welcome to Seafood Palace. How may I assist you today?" he asks, grinning at Alyssa.

"*How may I assist you today?* Really, Eric?" Alyssa smirks. "Aren't you supposed to just ask *how many in your party?*"

I look between the two of them, and make a mental note to ask Alyssa about this little exchange later.

"You know me. Always trying to keep it original," he says with a chuckle and a wink. "Would you ladies prefer to sit inside or outside? We have space heaters out there to help with the chill," he adds as he sees the expression on my face.

After considering it for a minute, and getting a nod from Alyssa, I say, "Outside please." It's such a beautiful day. I want to enjoy the sunshine on my face, the smell of fresh air, and the sound of the waves hitting the shore—even if it is a bit chilly. Eric leads us to a table on the patio overlooking Lake Superior. The view is spectacular—water stretching on for miles, a dozen long metal docks gleaming in the sunlight, and a lighthouse perched atop a small hill to be a guiding light. "Thank you," I say as Alyssa and I sit down.

"You're welcome. Your waitress will be with you shortly." He hands us our menus and turns to leave.

As soon as he walks away, and is out of earshot, I look at Alyssa. "Okay, *who* was that? And what was with that little conversation and look you two shared?"

Taking a sip of the water that the waitress just brought, Alyssa shrugs. "That's Eric. I met him a few years ago when I started coming here. We're friends."

"*Just* friends?" I ask with a small chuckle.

"Yes! Just friends," she says, sticking her tongue out at me. "His family owns this restaurant, and he helps out here from time to time, but he's actually a public safety officer—which means he deals with both police *and* fire. And you know I could never date someone in that line of work. I don't think I'd be able to handle that again," she says sadly.

I give her a sympathetic look, knowing that she lost her brother, who was a police officer who was killed in the line of duty. "Now it makes sense why you two are just friends."

"And he's actually a friend of Brandon Edwards, which is how I first heard about Edwards Mansion," she says, changing the topic.

"I see," I say with a nod. "So what's good here?" I glance at the menu, trying to decide which option sounds the best. Everything sounds amazing.

"I recommend the Lake Trout. It's mouthwateringly good! Plus, it's caught locally so it's super fresh."

"Perfect. That sounds great."

Alyssa and I order our food and sit quietly for a few minutes, just enjoying the view. "So," Alyssa finally breaks the silence, "are you ever going to tell me *exactly* what happened with you and Tim?"

"I don't want to talk about it. Let's just say that he made some bad decisions and got mixed up with some shady people. I was scared for my life, so I decided to run."

"Did that asshole *threaten* you?" she asks wide-eyed.

"Yeah, he did actually. That's why I knew I had to

get out of Arizona as fast as possible. Starting over in a new town just seemed like the safest option. And I doubt he has ever even heard of this town, so I shouldn't have to worry about him finding me. He obviously knows about you, of course, but I never shared any information with him about where you live."

"Thank goodness for that," Alyssa says.

Our food arrives and we quickly change topics as we dig in. "Mmmm—this is delicious!" I say happily as I chew a mouthful of trout. "You weren't kidding about the fish being fresh."

"I told you it was amazing. So, what were you thinking of buying for furniture? Maybe that will help determine where I should take you first," she says as she takes a bite of her food.

"Well, first things first, I need a bed. I'd like to get a couch and a kitchen table, too."

"What about dressers, TV, those kinds of things?"

"I can live without a dresser for now—my closet is pretty big—and as for the TV, I can just watch movies on my laptop for the time being. I need to find a job and save some more money before I start buying anything extra. I don't want to blow through all of the savings I have left after what I spent on the house and necessities."

"Fair enough," Alyssa says. "But you at least need

a lamp or two. There's a great discount store where we can find those and a few cool accessories for pretty cheap. And the Furniture Outlet is probably your best bet for finding an affordable bed and couch. As for the kitchen table and chairs, my neighbor has a nice one that she has been wanting to get rid of. I'm sure she'll give you a good deal."

"Awesome! That works for me."

We finish our meals as we make a plan of where to go first. After paying for our food, we say goodbye to Eric and head out to do some furniture shopping. I'm able to find everything that I'm looking for and by the time we're done I've placed orders and scheduled delivery days. "Not too bad. I should have everything delivered by Tuesday, so that means only a few days sleeping on the floor," I say.

"You're welcome to stay with me, Gabby, until your furniture arrives," Alyssa offers.

"Thank you, but no. I'd rather stay at my place and unpack all of the boxes before furniture arrives. Besides, I'll probably spend most of the weekend job hunting anyway."

"Sounds like fun," she says as I roll my eyes. "In that case, let's stop at the inn before you get lost in the help wanted ads." Alyssa turns the car onto the main road, and we drive until we come to the enormous inn.

It really *is* a mansion! It's a five-story tall brick building with turrets and balconies everywhere I look. A large water fountain in the middle of a shallow pool sits out front. Brick-paved walkways lead around the fountain and through a garden that will soon be blooming with bright, colorful flowers. Giant pillars frame the front door and smaller stone pillars sit at the corners of a large enclosed sun room. "Wow!" I exclaim breathlessly. "This place is phenomenal!"

"You haven't even seen all of it yet," says Alyssa as we park and step out of the car. "There are still lighted walking paths that wind around the entire property, a tennis court, and a vegetable garden. Not to mention a boat house and a separate gardener's cottage."

I look at her wide-eyed. "This is incredible. I've never seen anything like it."

As we're walking through the flower garden, I happen to notice a very attractive looking man talking on his cell phone near the edge of the fountain. He's tall, with short dark hair, and the most gorgeous butt I've ever seen—his fitted slacks hugging his butt in all the right places.

"Quit gaping," Alyssa says as she breaks me out of my stare. "That's Brandon—Brandon Edwards."

"*That's* Brandon Edwards?" I ask in astonishment.

"Yeah. What were you expecting—a middle-aged, grumpy old man?" she teases.

"I don't know *what* I was expecting. But certainly not a hot, hunky man of my dreams type of guy," I say.

"Well, he may be hot and hunky, but don't hold your breath. He hasn't dated, or even been *interested* in dating, in a couple of years."

"Why not?"

"No idea. I asked Eric about him when I first saw him, and all Eric would tell me was that Brandon hardly even looks at women these days. Something about an accident? But he wouldn't tell me anymore than that. You'd have to ask him."

Interesting. Why would an attractive man like Brandon stay single? And *what* accident? That's not something I'm likely to find out anytime soon, since I can't exactly just go up to him and say *Hi, I'm Gabby. I heard that you don't date because of some accident. What happened?*

My thoughts are interrupted when suddenly Brandon looks up and catches my gaze. My throat goes dry and my palms get sweaty as he walks towards Alyssa and I. How embarrassing to be caught staring at him. I've got to think of an excuse, and quick, before he reaches us.

*a*s I approach the two women, I notice the short, brunette go stiff and quickly look away from me. No doubt embarrassed that I caught her staring at me with those beautiful brown eyes. I smile to myself. "Hello, ladies. Welcome to Edwards Mansion. I hope you're both enjoying all of the—sights—the inn has to offer," I say with a smile as I glance again at the brunette. "I'm Brandon."

"Hi, Brandon," says that taller blonde woman, who I now recognize as Alyssa—the woman my best friend Eric introduced me to last year. "This is my friend, Gabby."

"Good to see you again, Alyssa. Nice to meet you, Gabby," I say as I extend a hand to each of them for a handshake.

"Nice to meet you, too," says Gabby. "This is a beautiful inn you have," she says as she looks around.

"Thank you. It's been in my family for generations."

"I've heard," she says shyly. "My realtor told me about this place."

"Your realtor?"

"Yeah, I just moved here. She was telling me about all of the places that I needed to see once I settle in."

"Well, in that case, welcome to Wilkins Harbor. I'm sure you'll love it here. However, if you ladies will excuse me, I have some work to do. But feel free to look around and enjoy the property." I briskly walk away in the direction of my office, stepping inside the inn and heading for the back room.

When I get to my desk, I pull out my chair and login to my computer. I just found out that one of my desk clerks is quitting, so I need to post some help wanted ads quickly. It's almost the end of spring and we are pretty slow right now, but by the time summer arrives the inn will be swamped with tourists. I need to hire a replacement sooner rather than later so that I can train him or her before our busy season.

Opening my word document, I type up the ad. *Help Wanted: Front Desk Clerk. No experience necessary. Please contact Brandon Edwards for more information.*

After adding my phone number and proofreading it, I upload it to all of the online job listing sites. I can't forget about the local newspaper, so I email them a copy, too. Deciding that it might be a good idea to post a couple on the bulletin boards around the inn, I print a few copies—there is a bulletin board in the lobby for any local announcements and another board out by our parking lot.

After grabbing the fliers from the printer, I head out to hang them up, making a quick stop at the front desk. "How's everything going today, Chloe?" I ask the young desk clerk.

"Everything's going well, Mr. Edwards. We've had a few calls for reservations and we have two check-ins today, but otherwise it's pretty slow."

"Excellent. Let me know if anything comes up."

"I will, Mr. Edwards," she replies as I pin one of the fliers to the lobby bulletin board.

As I make my way outside and towards the parking lot, I see Gabby walking along one of the paths with Alyssa. "Hi, again, ladies. Are you enjoying yourselves so far?"

"Yes, we are. Thank you," says Gabby.

"Did you have a chance to see the picnic area by the stream out back? It's one of the most visited places on the property."

"We did! It was great meeting you, but we were

actually on our way out. Everything here is so lovely, and I would like to stay longer, but unfortunately I need to get home. I have lots of unpacking to do, and I still need to search for a job this weekend."

This could be the answer to my problem. The position doesn't really require any experience since I will be training the person, and a formal interview is kind of unnecessary. "What kind of job are you looking for?"

"Anything, really. I just need a job to help me get back on my feet. I didn't have time to find something here before I moved, and the majority of my final paycheck from my last job, pretty much all just went towards my furniture."

"Well, if you don't mind working the occasional weekend, I was just about to post this flier on the bulletin board." I hand her the help wanted flier and she glances at it before turning her gaze to look up at me.

"You're hiring? Really?" she asks hopefully.

"Yes, really," I say with a laugh. "Are you interested?"

"Definitely!" Gabby says excitedly. "When would you need me to start?"

"As soon as possible."

"Well, I was hoping to finish unpacking this weekend, I have to sign my closing papers for my house on

Monday morning, and my furniture is being delivered on Tuesday. Would Wednesday be soon enough?"

"Wednesday will be perfect. Say—eight o'clock?"

"That'll work," she says.

"Perfect. I'll see you on Wednesday, then. Just come inside the inn when you get here and ask for me at the front desk. The dress code is pretty casual, I just ask that you don't wear anything too revealing and no jeans with holes in them."

"I think I can manage that. Thank you for the opportunity, Brandon. Or should I call you Mr. Edwards now?"

"Brandon is fine. To be honest, one of my other clerks calls me Mr. Edwards and it drives me crazy. I'm not *that* old—though I suppose I *am* older than she is."

"Brandon it is, then," Gabby says with a smile.

"Well, I will let you and Alyssa get on your way, but I'll see you Wednesday morning, Gabby," I say as I smile back at her.

"See you then," she says as the two women walk towards the parking lot.

I watch until I can no longer see them before turning to go back into the inn. As I walk past the front desk I remove the job listing flier from the bulletin board, and crumple it up as I head into my office. Gabby accepting the position has removed my earlier worry about not having enough staff for the summer season. Now I just have to focus on the usual day to day tasks that come with running this inn.

Sitting down at my desk, I send a quick email to pull the ad I just sent to the newspaper and take down the postings on the job sites before I unlock the filing cabinet drawer underneath my desk, and pull out the file with employee information forms. Sorting through the papers, I select multiple forms that I need Gabby to fill out when she arrives on Wednesday—her general information as well as emergency contact information. Setting those aside, I look over the employee schedule to make sure I have all of the upcoming shifts covered and see who's working each shift. I rearrange and schedule myself for a couple of the shifts, as I want to handle most of Gabby's training to make sure she is comfortable with everything before allowing her to work on her own.

As I'm about to start looking over the inn's weekly financial information, my phone chimes with a text message. Pulling it out of my pocket, I look at the screen and see a message from Eric.

Eric: You up for some Saturday night fun?
Me: What did you have in mind?

Eric: The usual.....go to Eagle Tavern, drink a few beers, eat some buffalo wings, check out the ladies.

I roll my eyes and chuckle to myself. Eric and I have gone to Eagle Tavern every Saturday night for the last year. He always *checks out the ladies,* but I know he only does it because he's trying to find someone to take his mind off of who he truly wants—Alyssa.

Me: Sure, sounds good. I'll see you there at the usual time.

Slipping my phone back into my pocket, I return my attention to the financial information in front of me. I enter all of the nightly bank deposit totals that occurred this week into the computer and run the weekly reports. After printing off a copy—I like to keep a paper copy as well as a digital one—I slip it into the financial reports folder in the filing cabinet and re-lock the drawer.

Now that all of my paperwork is complete I can spend the rest of the afternoon wandering around the grounds and relaxing. Standing up from my desk, I leave my office and head towards my private quarters in the back of the inn. My place—which is known as the owner's residence—is the size of a large apartment. The lower floor has the living room, kitchen, and dining room, while the upstairs has two large bedrooms and a bathroom.

Climbing the stairs, I head to my bedroom to change clothes into something more casual. I grab one of my favorite long-sleeve t-shirts and a pair of jeans, and pull them on before heading back downstairs to make a quick lunch. Looking in my refrigerator, I sigh and make a mental note to go to the grocery store later to restock. I grab a protein shake instead, and drink it while stepping out onto my private patio.

Even with the chill, I like to sit out here to take in the view at the back of the inn. This side of Edwards Mansion has one of the walking paths, and a small stream with a stone bridge across it. In the distance I can see the vegetable garden where our chef grows most of the fresh ingredients he uses to cook for the guests. During the summer months, I enjoy watching the colorful sunsets while relaxing out here.

This place has always been special to me. I remember visiting my grandparents all of the time when I was little and my grandfather letting me help out around the inn. I used to play out in the gardens, and run along the trails to go down to the water. Smiling at the memory, I finish my shake and decide to walk around the property—maybe down towards Lake Superior or else out by the gardener's cottage.

I wave to guests as I pass by them on the trails and make my way to a sitting area near the water. Benches are set up around a fire pit—a great spot where guests like to spend the cooler summer nights. I take a seat on one of the benches and gaze out at the water. I would sit out here all day, every day, to watch the ships come and go if I could. Thankfully, today I have some time to do just that until I have to leave to meet Eric.

When I arrive at Eagle Tavern, I walk in and find Eric sitting at a high-top table. "Hey, man. How's it going?" he asks as I take a seat.

"It's going good."

"Hi, guys! Do you want your usual?" the waitress, Kelly, asks as she walks over to our table when she sees me sit down.

"That would be great, Kelly. Thanks," I say.

"The benefits of being a regular here is that they always know our orders," Eric says with a grin as she walks away.

"It's definitely a plus. Unless, of course, I want to have something different."

Eric raises his eyebrow. "Like you would ever order something different."

"Yeah, you're right," I say with a laugh. "I never order anything besides the usual."

"So, how is everything going at the inn? Are you still looking for help?" Eric asks.

"No, actually. I was going to post some help wanted ads, but then I ran into Alyssa and a friend of hers. Turns out her friend was looking for a job."

"Oh yeah! Gabby!"

"You know Gabby?" I ask curiously.

"No, not really. But they did stop in at Seafood Palace for lunch."

"Ahh, I see. So—did you ask Alyssa out yet?" I tease.

Eric glares at me before taking a sip of his beer that Kelly brought over. "No. I told you—it's not going to happen."

"Come on man! I don't see why you won't just ask her out already," I say with a grin.

"So, anyways—Gabby seems cool," he says, quickly changing the topic.

I let him get away with the topic change, knowing that it's pointless to keep pressing him about it. He always denies that he wants to be more than friends with her. "Yeah, she seems really nice from the few minutes I've talked to her. I hired her, and she starts work on Wednesday."

"That's great! Now that she'll be working for you, you'll be seeing a lot of Gabby," Eric says with a smile.

"I know that look in your eyes, and I know what you're thinking. Like you said about Alyssa—it's not going to happen."

"Come on, Brandon. You haven't been with a woman in over two years. Don't you think it's about time you put yourself out there again?"

"No, I don't actually. So drop it," I say tersely. "Gabby will be my employee, nothing more."

Our buffalo wings arrive and we change our conversation to sports, town events, and plans for next weekend. I'm just glad to have a reprieve from Eric meddling with my love life—or lack of one. I haven't allowed myself to have feelings for a woman in a long time. Not since the accident. Not since my fiancée, Olivia, passed away.

"Earth to Brandon. You okay man?" Eric asks as he taps the table in front of me, breaking me out of my thoughts.

"Yeah, sorry. Guess I spaced out for a minute there."

"I was asking if you're planning on going to the

Countdown to Summer Music Festival that's happening in a couple of weeks?"

"Yeah, I might try to go on one of the nights at least. I'm working the morning or afternoon shifts for the next few weeks so I can train Gabby, but maybe I'll come afterwards. I do want to see the Friday night headlining band."

"Who's headlining on that Friday?" Eric asks.

"Keweenaw Country."

"Awesome! I love their music." Eric takes a sip of his beer before adding, "You should bring Gabby—show her what one of our small town events is like."

I glare at Eric before answering, "Don't push it."

Eric raises both his hands in surrender. "Alright, alright. Forget I said anything."

As we finish eating our wings and drinking our beers I can't help but think about what he said. Part of me knows he's right about it being time for me to put myself back out there and date again, but I just don't know if I can do it. Losing Olivia was the worst thing to happen to me, and I'm not sure if I'm ready to open my heart again. Even if I am, Gabby is my employee, and I refuse to date my employees.

Chapter Three

GABBY

I officially closed on my home on Monday, and all of my new furniture arrived yesterday. Everything fits perfectly into the house. I'm glad that I was able to find furniture so quickly. I didn't mind sleeping on the floor in a sleeping bag, but it was really nice to sleep in a bed last night. I was finally able to have a restful night of sleep, which is good, because I had to wake up early this morning. I'm having Miss Jones—the woman I bought the house from—over for breakfast before my first day of work at Edwards Mansion. I talked with her before closing, and she is such a nice older woman—she reminds me of my grandmother.

I'm so grateful to have found an opportunity to work at the inn. When I first arrived in Wilkins Harbor, I was worried about not being able to find a job. Back in Arizona, I was the head pastry chef at a restaurant. I wasn't sure if such a small town would have pastry chefs in addition to the regular chefs. The money from my savings and from my family will last for a little while, but I wondered how long I would be able to survive on it. Thankfully, now I don't need to worry about it. Being a front desk clerk isn't exactly the same as being head pastry chef, but at least it's something, and I'm grateful to have it.

I take a quick shower and get dressed. It's almost seven o'clock, and Miss Jones is due to arrive any minute. I wanted to do something nice for her to thank her for allowing me to close on the home early, so I invited her over when I saw her on Monday.

Opening the oven door, I pull out the freshly baked cinnamon rolls to let them cool before icing them. Just as I set a bowl of mixed fruit and a couple of plates on the table, the doorbell rings. When I open the door, I find a short grey-haired woman with stylish blue framed glasses standing on my doorstep. "Hi, Miss Jones," I say with a warm smile. "Come on in."

"Thank you, dear," she says as she steps inside. "Something smells delicious!"

I grin. "Cinnamon rolls!"

"Yum! You sure know how to make this old lady happy! I've got a sweet tooth."

"In that case, let's go sit down and eat." We walk over to the table, and Miss Jones takes a seat while I grab the pan of cinnamon rolls off of the counter. Grabbing the frosting and a spatula, I carry all of the items to the table and sit down. "Do you like a lot of frosting or a little frosting?"

"How about a medium amount of frosting? I don't want to overdo it, you know."

"Sounds good. Please help yourself to some fruit and coffee," I say as I spread the frosting onto a couple of the rolls.

"Are you liking it here so far?" asks Miss Jones as she takes a sip of coffee.

I give her a small smile. "Yeah, so far it's been really nice. This house has been perfect. I wanted to thank you again for allowing me to move in early."

"Oh, of course dear. Samantha said you were having some trouble with you ex, and needed the keys early. Now, I'm not sure what kind of troubles— and I don't expect you to tell me—but I know what it's like to deal with a dangerous relationship."

I swallow hard, feeling a bit emotional. "You do?"

"Oh yes." She gets a sad look in her eyes, and stares out the window at the water for a moment before continuing. "I shared this house with my ex-fiancé a long time ago. We were *so* in love, or so I thought, and I asked him to move in here with me

because I loved this house. He moved in, and everything was perfect for a while. Then, one day, we got
into an argument, and he beat me." She pauses and I
gently reach out to pat her hand. Miss Jones gives
me a lopsided smile. "Thankfully I was smart
enough to end things immediately. After he beat me
and stormed out, leaving me on the floor, I managed
to crawl to the phone and call the police. I also
called my dad to come over to stay with me in case
my fiancé came back, and my dad changed the
locks."

"I'm glad you were able to get out of that situation and ended up being alright."

"Me too. But after that day I couldn't bear to stay
in this house. I tried for a while, but it was too
painful. There were too many memories here—of
him and I together, of our love, and of that horrible
day that I'll never forget. So, I moved back in with
my parents until I found a new place."

"You never sold this house though?"

"No, I could never bring myself to do it. I rented
it out for a while, but that's it."

"So—why did you sell it to me?" I ask curiously.

Miss Jones smiles. "When Samantha mentioned
that she had someone looking to move to Wilkins
Harbor to make a fresh start, I knew I had to sell. I
know what it's like to give up everything and start

over, so it just felt right. I listed it for sale, and told Samantha to make sure that you saw the listing."

I can feel tears welling up in my eyes. "Well, I want you to know how grateful I am that you gave up something so special to you so that I could have the opportunity to start over in such a beautiful place."

"You're welcome."

We talk for a little while longer before the alarm on my cell phone chimes, interrupting our conversation. "I'm so sorry, Miss Jones, but I need to head to work. I don't want to be late for my first day."

"That's alright. I should get going anyway." She stands up, and gives me a hug before I walk her to the door. Before she leaves, she takes my hands in hers, and gives me a serious look. "One word of advice from an old lady, Gabby—don't make the same mistake I did. I let the fear of that horrible relationship keep me from truly experiencing love again. I could never bring myself to be with anyone else when I was younger, and only recently did I find someone again. Don't be afraid to put your heart out there, and let someone in again. You deserve to be happy, okay?"

With tears in my eyes, I pull her into another hug, and let the tears spill down my cheeks. "Thank you. I *promise* I'll give love another chance."

As we pull apart she opens the door to leave.

"Thank *you*—for making an old woman a breakfast to satisfy her sweet tooth." She winks at me and smiles.

"It was my pleasure. We'll have to do it again sometime."

"I'd love that."

I wave goodbye to Miss Jones as she walks to her car, before going back inside to grab my purse. I quickly jump into my SUV and head to the inn. Pulling into the parking lot, I find a spot in the employee parking section and pull into it. Climbing out of the car, I straighten my clothes and make sure that I look alright. I want to look at least somewhat professional on my first day on the job, even if it is casual attire.

Walking into the inn, I head straight to the front desk. "Welcome to Edwards Mansion. How can I help you?" asks the desk clerk.

"Hi. I'm here to see Brandon. I'm supposed to start work here today."

"Oh, you must be Gabby! I'll let Mr. Edwards know you're here." She picks up the phone to call for Brandon. "Mr. Edwards, Gabby is here." Hanging up the phone she says, "He'll be right up. You can put your things in here." She shows me a small closet behind the desk.

"Thanks." I put my purse and jacket into the closet before glancing around the lobby while I wait.

The inside of Edwards Mansion is just as breath-taking as the outside. From here in the lobby I can see beautiful windows decorated with pieces of stained glass, lush red carpets lining the floors, and walls that are made of a gorgeous polished wood. The antique chandelier hanging in the middle of the lobby is exquisite, and adds a touch of charm to the inn.

"Good morning, Gabby," Brandon says as he walks into the lobby. "How are you on this beautiful morning?"

"I'm fine, thanks," I say with a smile.

"Alright. First things first—let me give you a tour of the inn. That way you'll be more familiar with where things are, and I can give you a little background about the place."

"That would be great."

"Alright then, this way," he says as he begins to walk towards the hallway. "Edwards Mansion was built in 1905 by my great-great grandfather. It started out as a family home, but my grandparents turned it into an inn about fifty years ago. It sits on twenty-two-acres, has forty rooms, and a private owner's quarters."

"Wow, that's incredible!" I say in awe as we continue down the hallway. "How many floors are there?"

"There are five floors. The guest rooms are on

floors two through five. This first floor has the lobby, my office, a kitchen, a dining area, laundry room, a library, a music room, a sitting room, and access to the sun room."

Brandon leads me into the first room. "This is the library," he says.

There are a couple of arm chairs, as well as a couch and an antique writing desk. The shelves stretch from floor to ceiling along the walls and are lined with hundreds of books. I run my fingers along the spines of the books as I walk down the row, glancing at the titles. "These are all for guests?" I ask.

"Yes. Guests are free to come in and borrow books whenever they wish. They just have to sign them out at the front desk. All we ask is that the historical books about Edwards Mansion stay in this room, but guests are welcome to look at them in here."

"That makes sense," I say with a nod. "You wouldn't want those books to get lost. I imagine they're not easy to find."

"No, they're not. A lot of them only have this one copy in existence," Brandon says. We head out of the library and to the next room down the hall. "This is the music room. We updated it a few years ago to add a bit of soundproofing to the walls. It's not used too much, but every now and then we will have a guest come in here to play." In the middle of the room sits a stunning Steinway grand piano. "Do you play?" Brandon asks.

"No," I say sadly. "I always wanted to take piano lessons as a child, but my parents couldn't afford it at the time, and when they could have afforded it, I was too busy with school and sports. Do *you* play?"

"I used to—a long time ago," he says with a half smile and a sad look in his eyes. I want to ask why he doesn't play anymore, but I don't want to pry.

Brandon leads me further down the hall to show me the kitchen and dining room before leading me into the sun room. Each room is more impressive than the last. "Oh, wow. This room must have gorgeous views in the summer," I say as I step inside. The sun room overlooks the gardens and one of the walking paths, with Lake Superior in the background.

"It *does* have a great view, especially when all of the flowers are blooming. It's also a great place to read one of those books our guests can borrow from the library." We make our way back down the hallway and to the stairs. "Usually all of our rooms are full, but since this is our slow season, most of the rooms are empty. Let me show you a couple of them."

"Are all of them the same?" I ask.

"No, they're not, actually. Each of the rooms has

its own decor. They all have a similar feel, but slightly different."

"Are they decorated with modern decor or do they still have that historical look?"

Brandon smiles. "They're all still historical—with a few modern upgrades such as lamps and televisions, of course—but my grandmother insisted that the inn keep its historical charm."

He unlocks the first door at the top of the stairs and pushes it open. Stepping inside, I look around in awe at all of the historical touches. Wall sconces line the walls—adding additional lighting to the lamps— with electricity now replacing the candles they once held. In the corner of the room is an antique desk, and an intricately carved book shelf. A wood fireplace is on one wall with historical photos of Edwards Mansion hanging above the mantle. In the center of the room is a large four-poster canopy bed with a small table on each side. The ceiling has elegant crown moulding, and a long bench runs along the length of the wall of windows, providing a window seat. A decent sized bathroom with a claw-foot tub, and a modern walk-in corner shower completes the room.

"This is incredible, Brandon. I feel like I walked back in time a little."

"I'm glad you like it," he says as he leads me out

and to another room. This one is similar to the first, but has its own unique design touches. After seeing a few more rooms, I follow Brandon back downstairs and to his office. "Now that you've had a tour of the inside, I need you to fill out some paperwork for me before we start your training. Please take a seat." He motions to the chair opposite his and I sit down. He sits down in his chair and slides a couple of papers across his desk. "Just your basic information and emergency contact information," he says as I glance at the documents in front of me.

I fill out the required forms and pass them back to Brandon. "Excellent," he says. "Now, you met Chloe at the front desk this morning. I plan on handling most of your training, but I want you to shadow her for today. I've arranged the schedule so that I'll be working with you for the rest of the week." He hands me a copy of the schedule. "Just let me know in advance if you need any particular days off or any changes made."

"Okay, will do."

Brandon walks with me out to the front desk. "Chloe, please show Gabby the ropes. How to make a reservation in the computer, how to mark a room for housekeeping, all of the basics."

"Yes, Mr. Edwards," Chloe says.

I cover my giggle with a cough, remembering how

Brandon mentioned the other day that he hates being called Mr. Edwards. Brandon smiles at me and shakes his head as he makes his way back towards his office.

"How was your tour?" Chloe asks.

"It was great! This place is truly amazing."

"Yeah, it really is a beautiful place, and I love working here. Mr. Edwards is such a great boss."

"Well, that's good to know," I say.

"Let me show you how our computer system works. It's pretty simple." Chloe walks me through the steps of making a reservation and cancelling a reservation, as well as how to make sure house-keeping knows which rooms need to be cleaned. She also shows me how to check guests in when they arrive and check them out when they leave. Overall, everything seems pretty easy and straightforward. Nothing I can't handle. Chloe assures me that I won't be scheduled to work alone until I'm comfortable with everything.

Looking at the schedule I received earlier, I see that shifts are eight hours long—a morning shift, an afternoon shift, and a night shift, with a half hour for break during each shift. "How does break time work if we're running the desk?" I ask.

"Well, we have a break time so that we can eat, but if someone comes to the desk, or the phone rings, we have to pause our break and come back to it when we're finished helping the customers."

"How often are each of the desk clerks scheduled for night shift?"

"Not very often. Mr. Edwards doesn't always schedule a night shift. There's usually no one that arrives that late, and there are usually no phone calls. The doors lock at midnight, so anyone who isn't already checked in and in possession of a key needs to ring the doorbell. Mr. Edwards has it set up so that he will hear it in his private quarters—which means he takes care of it himself. The only time we really have night shifts is during the summer months," Chloe explains.

"Why is that?" I ask.

"Because summer is our busiest season and late arrivals are more common."

"That makes sense," I say.

The rest of my shift is spent mostly visiting with Chloe since it's pretty slow. A few guests check in and there are a few phone calls for reservations, but that's it. As I'm preparing to leave after my shift is over, Brandon ventures back into the lobby. "How was your first day, Gabby?"

"It was great, thanks."

"Good to hear. Have a good rest of your day and I'll see you tomorrow. I'll be working with you at the desk. We're scheduled for the afternoon shift—I want you to get a feel for each of the different shifts. They're all pretty much the same, although on a typical morning shift you will also count and record the money from the night before and bring it to me. The afternoon shift is responsible for refilling everything in the dining area and common bathrooms."

"That sounds good. I definitely want to see what each of the shifts are like. I'll see you tomorrow. Bye, Chloe!" I wave to both of them as I make my way out the door to head home. I smile to myself as I walk to my car. My first day of work in my new town was fantastic. The inn is gorgeous, and everyone I met today seemed really friendly. I can definitely get used to this new life.

Chapter Four

BRANDON

"*D*id you have any issues working with her?" I ask Chloe as soon as Gabby leaves.

"No, not at all! Gabby was great, Mr. Edwards!" Chloe says happily.

"Did she seem to understand how everything works with our computer system?"

"Yeah, she caught on quickly with the computer system. I think she'll be a good fit here."

"That's excellent to hear, and it's all I needed to know. Thanks, Chloe. Have a good rest of your day."

"Thanks! You too, Mr. Edwards."

I give Chloe a quick nod before turning to head to my apartment for the evening. Checking my watch as I arrive at my door, I see that it's just after four o'clock. Plenty of time for me to eat dinner and relax before bed.

Going into the kitchen I reheat a piece of leftover lasagna in the microwave and grab a bottle of beer from the refrigerator. I carry my dinner into the living room and set it on the coffee table. I take a seat in the middle of the couch, and turn on the TV. Flipping through the channels I find a movie to watch until the baseball game comes on later tonight.

As I'm finishing up my dinner the phone rings. "Hello?" I say as I answer the call.

"Hello, dear. Are you busy?"

"Oh hi, Grandma! No, I'm not busy."

"Oh, good. I was just calling to see how you're doing. How's everything going at the inn?" she asks.

"I'm doing pretty good. Everything here is going great. Slow though—like it usually is this time of year."

"Ah, well, don't worry—business will pick up soon. Only a couple of weeks until May and then the summer season will start."

"Summer doesn't start until June, Grandma," I tease.

"Technicalities!" she says with a chuckle. "Summer season at the inn always starts in May. I remember it was always busy starting with the week of the *Countdown to Summer Music Festival*."

"It still is busy that week. We're almost fully booked, actually."

"That's good to hear. Do you have enough staff to handle it? I know you don't like to schedule anyone for the late night shifts, but you can't be there all by yourself during the busy season—you'll go crazy running back and forth from your apartment at all hours of the night," she says.

"Don't worry. I've got enough staff to cover all of the shifts and still give everyone a couple of days off each week. I just hired a new desk clerk to replace the one that quit," I assure her.

"I was wondering about that—I heard a few days ago that you lost someone."

"Yeah, thankfully someone I know has a friend that just moved to town and she was looking for a job."

"That's great sweetie. Well, I won't keep you any longer—I'm sure you've got better things to do than talk to your grandma all night. But before I let you go, your grandpa and I would like to have you over for dinner sometime soon. Let me know when you're free, okay?"

"That would be great. You know I can't pass up one of your home cooked meals!"

Grandma laughs. "Yes, I was counting on that."

"I'll be sure to check my calendar soon to see when I'm available and let you know. I'd love to get together with you and Grandpa as soon as I can. I haven't seen you in a while—at least not for more than a few minutes."

"I'm looking forward to seeing you soon. Love you, Brandon."

"Love you too, Grandma," I say as I hang up the phone. I quickly get up and carry my dirty dishes into the kitchen to rinse them before placing them in the dishwasher. Walking back into the living room, I stretch out on the couch and flip to the baseball game on TV, prepared to relax for the rest of the night.

I wake up to a dreary, rainy morning. If the weather stays like this, Gabby and I can expect most of the guests to be inside this afternoon, which means I should schedule some indoor activities for us to offer them. Which also means I need to make an announcement to the guests that there will be new options available to them.

Crawling out of bed, I take a quick shower and get dressed before heading downstairs and over to the main area of the inn. As I walk into the lobby I grab a cup of coffee from the coffee station in the corner, and make my way over to the dining room where most of the guests are finishing breakfast at the long family-style tables. I can smell the delicious aromas of freshly baked cinnamon rolls as I enter.

"Good morning everyone," I say cheerfully. "I just want to let you all know that since the weather isn't very nice, we'll be planning some indoor activities for this afternoon. I'll post a flyer on the bulletin board out by the front desk as soon as I can with a list of options. You're all welcome to join in if you'd like."

"That's so nice of you!" says one guest named Mrs. O'Leary.

"We were all just talking about how long this day was going to feel while we sit in our rooms doing nothing. What kind of activities are you talking about, sonny? Not playing those crazy video games you kids play these days, I hope, " Mr. O'Leary says warily.

"Pay no attention to him. He's just a grouchy old man," teases Mrs. O'Leary.

"The activities aren't all going to be *lame*, are they?" asks a teenage girl sitting next to her parents.

"Natalie! Don't be rude!" scolds her mother. "So sorry about that Mr. Edwards."

"Please, call me Brandon. And don't worry," I say with a chuckle, "there will be something for everyone to enjoy. I promise you won't find all of the options *lame* Natalie, and I'll make sure there is something besides video games, Mr. O'Leary."

"Thank you so much for providing us all with options. It'll make the day less gloomy," says another guest named Jill.

"You're welcome. It's all part of the job. I'll let you all enjoy the rest of your breakfast," I say with a smile as I turn to leave the room. As I walk towards my office, I run through a list of possible options in my head. I have some board games at my place that I can bring to the sunroom and a couple of movies that guests can choose from, although I should probably see if Gabby can bring a few extra—the movies I have are mostly old westerns and a few action films. The ladies may want some chick flick options. We also have the library and music room available.

Stepping into my office I pull my cell phone out of my pocket and click on Gabby's number from my speed dial list. She answers after a couple of rings. "Hello?"

"Hi, Gabby. Sorry to bother you at home. I didn't wake you did I?"

"No, you didn't wake me. What's up?" she asks.

"I was just wondering if you can bring a couple of movies with you when you come to work this afternoon. Since it's raining today I wanted to provide activities for the guests. I have some movies that I'm going to bring, but I was hoping you would have a couple of options in another genre—I've got westerns and action."

"Sure, I can do that. I'll bring a few of my favorite dramas and comedies," Gabby says cheerfully. "Luckily I just unpacked those the other day, so I know right where they are."

"That'll be great, thanks. I was also wondering if you had any other ideas for activities. I've come up with movies and board games. Plus there is the library and music room. But I was thinking we should have another option or two. We have a wide range of guest ages today, and I was hoping to provide options for everyone."

"How about baking?" she asks. "They can use the inn's kitchen, and I can bring some of my grandmother's recipes."

"Huh—I've never thought of that before. That's pretty brilliant! I can bring some of my grandma's favorite recipes too, and I'll make sure the refrigerator is stocked with all of the necessary ingredients we'll need for baking."

"Is there anything else you need me to bring?"

"No, I think that should be it. Unless there is something specific that you think you'll need for any of the recipes that won't be here already. I'll see you in a couple of hours."

"Sounds great. See you soon, Brandon."

"Alright, bye Gabby," I say as I hang up.

I sit down at my desk and turn on my computer to make a flier to post with the activities list. I print a copy and bring it out to the bulletin board by the front desk before heading to the kitchen to check what ingredients I need to pick up for baking. Making a quick note of what I need to buy, I head back to my apartment to gather up the games and movies. After bringing the games to the sunroom and the movies to the sitting room, I walk out to my truck and drive to the grocery store.

When I arrive, I pull out my list and find everything we'll need for the baking this afternoon. I decide to grab a few extra groceries as well, such as popcorn and a variety of candy for the movies. I'm not sure what everyone likes, so I keep it simple with several kinds of chocolate candy bars, some sweet and sour candies, and some mints.

Once I've gone through the check-out and paid for the groceries, I load them into my truck and head back to Edwards Mansion. Since it's raining I decide to park in my private driveway instead of the main parking lot and go through my apartment to bring the groceries to the inn. Just as I step inside, my cell phone rings. I quickly set the bags of groceries down on my kitchen counter and pull my phone out of my pocket. I see that it's Gabby calling. "Hey, Gabby. What's up?"

"Hey, Brandon. Um—I really hate to ask, but Alyssa is working and I don't really know anyone else here yet. I was out running some errands before work, and my car died. I had it towed to the shop, but they don't have any rental cars so now I'm stuck here. Would you mind coming to pick me up? I'd need to run home to grab a few things first, but then I could just come back to the inn with you and chill there until our shift starts. I can have Alyssa come pick me up after work to bring me home," she says all in a rush.

"Gabby, calm down. I don't mind. I just have to put the groceries in the kitchen and then I'll be right there. Which shop are you at?" I ask.

"I'm at Tony's Repair Shop."

"Okay. I'll see you in a few minutes."

"Thanks, Brandon. I really appreciate it," Gabby says.

"It's really no problem."

I hang up the phone and grab the groceries off of the counter. I quickly bring them down to the kitchen at the inn and put them away before heading back out to my truck to go pick up Gabby. When I arrive at Tony's Repair Shop I see Gabby standing in the doorway with her hot pink rain coat. I pull up as close to the door as I can so that she doesn't have to run very far in the rain. Leaning over the seat, I pull the door handle to open the door for her and she quickly jumps in.

"Hi!" she says with a shy smile. "Thanks for picking me up. I wasn't sure what I was going to do. I thought about just calling a taxi, but I thought I'd see if you were available first."

"Nah. No need for a taxi. You said you needed to run home first?" I ask.

"Yes, please. I need to grab those recipes and drop these bags off."

"Just tell me where to go."

"It's the little blue bungalow on the corner of Elliott Street and Fort Wells Drive," she says cheerfully.

"Really? I know that house. It used to belong to a friend of my grandparent's—Miss Jones."

"Miss Jones is a friend of your grandparents? This really *is* a small town!" Gabby says with a laugh.

I laugh too. "Yeah, it really is."

Turning down Elliott Street, I take a left onto Fort Wells Drive and pull up into the driveway of Gabby's bungalow. "I just have to run in quick, but you're welcome to come in if you want," she says.

"Sure. I'll come in for a minute."

Gabby smiles as she quickly hops out of the truck

and runs for her front door. I follow behind and reach the front door just as she unlocks it and pushes it open. As we step inside, I take my shoes off by the door and look around. "Wow, I love what you've done with this place in such a short period of time," I say.

"Thanks! I still have a few things to put away and move around, but I'm almost done." Gabby walks into her kitchen to put her bags down and grabs a small box off of the counter. She pulls a bag of apples and some cookie cutters out of one of the bags and comes back into the entryway.

"Do you need to put the rest of your groceries away?" I ask, eyeing the other bags in the kitchen.

"Huh?" she asks following my gaze. "Oh! No, everything else is fine on the counter until later. Nothing needs to be refrigerated. I'm all set."

"Easy enough. We still have a couple of hours before our shift, though. Are you sure you don't want me to come back to pick you up later?"

"Nah, I don't want to inconvenience you any more today. I'll just go sit in the library and read or some-thing until it's time to start work. No big deal," she replies.

"It wouldn't be an inconvenience, but if that's what you want to do, that's fine too," I say with a smile as we head back outside. "Can you believe this rain? It's raining even harder now than it was when we arrived here!"

"I know, right?!" Gabby tucks an old small box under her coat as she hustles to my truck.

As we drive back to the inn I nod towards Gabby's hands and ask, "So—what's in that box?"

"It's my grandmother's recipe box," she says fondly. "She gave it to me before I left Arizona."

"Is that where you're from?" I ask.

"Yeah. I lived there for most of my life until I went away to college."

"Wow. What brought you all the way from Arizona to Wilkins Harbor?"

The color drains from Gabby's face as she turns and stares out the window. I see her clenching and unclenching her fists in her lap. She reaches up and swipes at her eyes.

"Oh—um—I'm sorry. You don't have to tell me. It's none of my business," I say as I realize it seems like a touchy subject. The rest of the drive to the inn is very quiet as I keep my eyes on the road and Gabby continues to sit silently, staring out the window.

Chapter Five

GABBY

As I sit on the couch in the library at the inn, I stare at the book on my lap, and think about how abruptly conversation between Brandon and I ended on the way here. Hopefully he doesn't think I'm rude for never answering his question, but I just couldn't bring myself to tell him about Tim. I feel so stupid for having trusted such an evil man. I don't want my new boss to think he hired a crazy person.

As I take a sip of my hot tea, and a deep breath, I can't help but have my thoughts drift back to that awful day.

I can hear voices booming from inside my apartment as I turn my key in the lock. That can mean only one thing—Tim has his new friends over again. There's just something about his friends that makes me feel uneasy. Whenever he comes home after hanging out with them he's different—he's angry and jumpy. It's very concerning, and I need to get away from him, far away. He's starting to scare me, which is why I plan on leaving him as soon as I can close on my new house in Michigan.

As I step through the door I hear them talking in the kitchen. "When is this job happening?" Tim asks.

"It's going down tomorrow night," one of his friends says. "The truck carrying over a hundred grand is scheduled to arrive at the bank around midnight. We're going intercept it before it gets there. There's two security guards in the front and one in the back with the cash."

"How many of us?" asks Tim.

"It's the three of us and my buddy John," says another friend.

I stand frozen in the doorway at what I hear, my heart racing. What the hell has Tim gotten himself into? All I can think about is that I need to get out of here fast—before they realize I'm here. Just as I turn to run back out the door, I hear an angry voice yell behind me. "What the hell are you doing here? You're not supposed to be home yet!" Tim barks.

"I—I—finished work early," I stammer quickly, barely able to utter the words.

Tim storms over and backs me up against the door, placing his hands on either side of my head, his face only inches away from mine. "What did you hear?"

I can feel his cold eyes pierce into me like daggers as I

stiffen up in fear. "I didn't—" I shake my head. "I didn't hear anything," I finally blurt out as I hold back tears.

"I doubt that." Tim lowers his voice, and leans closer to me to stare into my eyes. I close my eyes tight as I feel his face move to the side of my head. I feel his hot breath on my ear as he brushes my hair off from the side of my face, and I bite the inside of my cheek to keep myself from whimpering. "Whatever you heard, you damn well better keep your mouth shut. I'm warning you—if you say one word about what you heard to anyone, you're dead. I'll kill you myself, you got that?" he whispers into my ear with a slow, calm tone.

I nod my head yes very quickly as I stand visibly shaking, pushing myself harder up against the door, and as far away from Tim as possible. My heart feels like it's going to beat out of my chest—I'm so scared. He pushes himself back after giving me a kiss on my cheek, and he lets out an evil chuckle. "Now—be a good girl and go upstairs until the guys leave."

I finally open my eyes as I run up the stairs to the bedroom as fast as I can, locking the door behind me and leaning against it. After taking a few deep breaths I grab my cell phone and walk into the bathroom. After locking the bathroom door, I turn on the shower and the sink faucet to muffle any sounds before dialing my realtor's number. "Samantha? I need your help," I say as I try to keep the terror out of my voice.

Shaking my head, I try to once again bury the thoughts of that day out of my head. I take a deep breath to calm myself, and finally glance at my watch to see that I have about ten minutes left until I need to be ready to work. Closing my eyes, I pinch the bridge of my nose and hang my head. I need to pull it together before I head to the front desk. I hear someone clear their throat, and I look up to see Brandon standing in the doorway.

"Hey. Are you alright?" he asks in a caring, soothing tone.

Letting out a sigh I slowly say, "Yeah, I'm fine." I straighten up, and pull myself together. "I was just about to come out to the front desk."

"I'm sorry if I brought up something painful earlier in the car. I didn't mean to pry," Brandon utters.

"No, it's alright. It's just not something I like to talk about," I answer as I regain my composure.

"I understand. We all have *something* we don't like to talk about, right? Come on, let's go start some activities," he says nodding towards the hallway.

Standing up from the couch, I put the book back on the shelf and follow Brandon out front to see which guests are interested in each of the activities. We decide that I will be in charge of helping with the baking and he will set up the movies and board games. When we get to the front desk we find several of the guests waiting in the lobby and a few more making their way down the stairs. "Hi, everyone!" I say cheerfully with a small wave.

"Did everyone have a chance to look at the activities list?" Brandon asks.

"I think we all did," says Mrs. O'Leary as she looks around to nods of agreement from all of the other guests.

"Perfect," says Brandon. "Now, what is everyone interested in doing?"

"I've been looking forward to the baking all day!" says Mrs. O'Leary excitedly.

"Me too!" exclaims another guest, Mrs. Anderson.

"Not me," says Jill sheepishly. "I always burn everything. I'd rather watch a movie."

"I'll take whoever wants to bake to the kitchen with me," I say happily. Mrs. O'Leary, Mrs. Anderson, and another guest named Evelyn all join me where I stand off to one side.

"Anyone else for the movie?" Brandon asks as he looks around.

"I love movies!" says Natalie. Her mom Sarah and another guest named Jake join the movie group with her.

Natalie's dad Alan asks, "Does anyone else want to play board games with me?"

"I always love a little competition," says Mr. O'Leary.

"Count me in," says Mr. Anderson with a grin.

"Excellent! Now that we have our groups—bakers follow Gabby to the kitchen, board games are in the sun room, and I'll get the movie set up in the sitting room. If anyone wants to switch activities at any point, feel free to do so," Brandon says. "Gabby, you just worry about the baking for now. I'll answer the phone and handle any new arrivals. When you ladies are done, we can all take a break to eat. After dinner you can come help at the desk."

"Sounds good," I say with a smile. "Just let me know if you need me for anything."

"I will," he says.

As everyone else wanders off to their activities, I lead the small group of women into the kitchen. "Is there anything specific you ladies want to bake today?" I ask.

"Nope. I just love baking—I'll make anything," says Mrs. Anderson. "My husband loves everything that I bake, but maybe he just likes sweets!"

"I don't know any recipes by heart, but I was hoping the rest of you might be able to share a recipe," says Evelyn.

"Of course! I brought a whole box full of my grandmother's recipes and I think Brandon brought a few of his as well. You're welcome to choose any of those," I say.

"Great!" she says cheerfully.

"How are we doing this?" asks Mrs. O'Leary. "Are we all baking the same thing or can we each bake something different?"

"That's entirely up to you. We can all work together on something or we can make a variety of desserts to share with everyone."

"Mmm....I love desserts," says Mrs. Anderson with a grin. "We should all make something different so we can sample a little bit of everything and share with the others."

"Sounds good to me," says Mrs. O'Leary.

"Me too," says Evelyn.

"Alright then, everyone choose something they want to bake," I say. "We have this entire side of the kitchen to use as long as we stay out the cook's way." The ladies all make a plan of what they want to do and start to gather their ingredients.

"What are you making, Gabby?" Evelyn asks.

I smile. "I'm making my grandmother's famous Caramel Apple Pie."

"That sounds delicious!" she says.

"That it is. It was always my favorite dessert as a little kid. My grandmother still makes it every Thanksgiving."

"Those must be some special memories for you, dear," says Mrs. O'Leary.

"Yeah, they really are," I say fondly. "I remember my grandmother letting me help her one Thanksgiving. I was feeling sad about something, and she brought me into her kitchen. She had me help her gather the ingredients, and then she walked me through the recipe step by step. The whole time, we were singing silly songs and laughing." The memory brings a big smile to my face.

We all spend the next couple of hours measuring and mixing ingredients to create delicious desserts to accompany tonight's dinner, which is being prepared by the cook and his assistants, on the other side of the kitchen. Between the four of us, we've made Caramel Apple Pie, Swiss Chocolate Cake, Chocolate Chip Cookies, and a Blueberry Pie. "These all look absolutely delicious! Great job everyone," I say with a smile. "Let's bring these out to the dining room."

We carry our creations into the dining room and set them on the buffet table along the wall. Just as we set the last dessert down, the other guests walk in followed by Brandon. They're all chatting amongst themselves—talking excitedly about something that happened in the movie and teasing each other about who ended up victorious in their games.

"Something smells amazing in here," says Brandon

as he sniffs the air. "Looks like you ladies have been busy."

"Thanks!" I say. "We worked hard to bake some of our favorites for everyone to enjoy."

Everyone gathers around the long table as the cook and his assistants bring dinner in, and set it down for a family style dinner. The savory aromas of the chicken dish and spicy corn waft through the air, making my mouth water. Mashed potatoes, coleslaw, and rolls complete the array of food spread out on the table.

"Alright, everyone. I hope you all had a wonderful day today. If you'll excuse us, we'll let you eat your dinner," Brandon says as he and I turn to leave.

"Why don't you two join us?" asks Mrs. O'Leary.

"That's very kind of you, but we really should get back to work," Brandon says.

"Oh, nonsense!" Mrs. O'Leary says as she waves her hand in a dismissive motion. "You've both been working all day. Besides, all of the guests are right here, and I know you have a bell if someone new comes."

Brandon looks at me, and I shrug. "Ok, sure. Why not," Brandon says.

We both walk around the table to the open seats next to Mrs. O'Leary. Brandon pulls a chair out for me, and I sit down. "Thank you," I say with a smile.

"You're welcome," he says with a nod as he takes the seat next to me. I shiver as his knee brushes against mine.

Once we're all seated, we begin to pass the food around the table. "How were the games?" asks Sarah.

"These boys gave me some good competition," says Alan.

"Who are you calling boys, sonny? We're both old enough to be your dad!" says Mr. O'Leary as he motions between himself and Mr. Anderson. Everyone around the table starts laughing.

"Fair enough," Alan says with a chuckle. "But you're both still as competitive as teenagers."

"Just because we're old doesn't mean we don't play to win," says Mr. Anderson with a smile.

"Alright, alright," says Mrs. Anderson as she waves her hand in the air. "Enough of that. How was the movie?" she asks turning towards Natalie.

"It was great! We were going to watch one of the comedies, but then Jake found a Western that I remember always watching with my grandpa, so we watched that instead," says Natalie.

"What about you girls? It looks like you baked a lot of goodies. Did you have a good time?" asks Jill.

"Oh, it was wonderful!" gushes Evelyn. "We shared lots of great memories while making the best meal of all—dessert!"

"Speaking of dessert," says Brandon, "let's have some!"

We all nod in agreement and stand up to go to the dessert table. Everyone decides to try a little piece of everything as we sit back down with our plates full of cake, pie, and cookies. There's collective agreement around the table as everyone savors their treats. "These are all delicious!" says Sarah. "Who made what?"

"Mrs. O'Leary made the Swiss Chocolate Cake and Mrs. Anderson made the Blueberry Pie. Evelyn made the Chocolate Chip Cookies and I made the Caramel Apple Pie," I say.

"Well you all did a wonderful job," says Jake.

"Gabby, you made the Caramel Apple Pie?" Brandon asks as he takes another bite.

"Mm-hmm," I say with a nod.

"I've never tasted anything so amazing!"

"Have you ever thought about baking professionally, dear," asks Mrs. O'Leary.

"Well—" I hesitate for a moment before continuing. "I was actually the head pastry chef at a restaurant in Arizona before I moved here."

Brandon's eyes shoot my way. "You were?"

I nod my head yes.

"That gives me an idea," he says excitedly. "How

would you feel about being a pastry chef here at the inn?"

I stare at him in shock, my mouth opening and closing. When I finally regain my voice I ask, "Really?"

"Yes really," he says with a chuckle.

"But—I thought you needed me as a desk clerk."

"I do, but I could work something out in the schedule to allow you to do both without having to work too much extra. Or I could look for another desk clerk. Some amazing desserts could really help to keep this inn on the list of popular destinations in the area."

"I can do both. I would love to be the pastry chef here!"

"Okay then," Brandon says with a smile. "I'll talk to the chef, and let him know you'll be taking over the baking."

I sigh happily as I finish off the last few bites of my dessert. It's going to feel great being able to bake professionally again, and I'm grateful to Brandon for giving me this opportunity.

Once we've finished dessert, Brandon and I excuse ourselves to go manage the front desk while the guests stay in the dining room and continue to visit. "Well, I'd say our rainy day activities were a success," Brandon says as we walk to the desk.

"Yeah, I think all of the guests had a really great time," I say with a smile. "Is an activity day something that you offer on a regular basis here at Edwards Mansion?"

"Not always. But ever since my grandparents owned the inn we've tried to provide a unique experience for our guests. Especially since we have a lot of guests that come here regularly. If you couldn't tell, we try to make everyone feel like they are a part of our family," Brandon says.

"Yeah, I've noticed. I know I've only been working here for a couple of days, but I enjoy it because it's not like anywhere I've ever been before. I've never stayed at a place where the hotel staff knows you by name and the guests know the staff as well. It's nice," I say. "And I mean it, it really *is* nice to be a part of something that feels like one big family. I'm liking Wilkins Harbor more each day that I'm here, especially Edwards Mansion."

"I'm glad you are enjoying it here. You've been a great addition to our staff so far. The guests really seem to like you, too."

"Well, that's good to hear," I say with a laugh. "I would hate to be *unlikeable*."

Brandon chuckles. "I highly doubt anyone would ever find *you* unlikeable."

As we sit at the desk the guests filter out of the

dining room, and stop to say a quick goodnight as they make their way to their rooms. They all thank us again for such a wonderful day of activities, and I can't help but feel blessed. We finish off the rest of our shift with a few late check-ins and one new walk-in guest before I say goodnight to Brandon and head home.

It was so fun being back in the kitchen baking again! And I can't wait to share more recipes of mine with the guests.

Chapter Six

BRANDON

I lock the doors to the inn behind Gabby as she leaves. Since it's not our busy season yet I don't have anyone scheduled for the front desk. I have a monitor in my apartment to alert me if anyone comes to the doors and if any guests happen to need assistance during the night there is a special call button.

After unlocking the door to my apartment, I switch on the lights and step inside. I make sure that the monitor for the front door is turned on before heading into the kitchen, and mixing myself a Jack and Coke. It's past midnight and I *should* head to bed, but after my day with Gabby I need to unwind a bit first. Being around her does something to me—it makes me feel things that I'd rather not feel at all anymore. And our conversation in the car earlier worries me. What is she hiding? She seemed alright when we were with the guests tonight, but when we were driving to the inn this afternoon she stopped talking when I asked what brought her to Wilkins Harbor.

I shouldn't be worrying about Gabby—or worrying about whatever it is she's hiding either—but I can't help it. She makes me want to care for someone again. And that scares the hell out of me. Glancing at my watch, I see that it's already twelve forty-five. I drink the last of my drink, and put the glass into the dishwasher before turning off the lights and heading upstairs.

After changing into my pajamas I climb into bed and lie awake, staring at the ceiling, trying to push all thoughts of Gabby out of my head. I try to think about what I need to do tomorrow—hoping it will help me fall asleep. The schedule for next week needs to be made and I promised my grandma that I would come for dinner. No matter what I try to think about, my thoughts keep returning to Gabby.

I spend the next couple of hours tossing and turning until the monitor alerts me that someone is at the door to the inn. Looking at the bright green numbers on the clock on my nightstand, I see that it's three in the morning. Grabbing my bathrobe, I wrap it around myself as I walk out of my apartment and through the inn to the main door. When I reach the door I look through the peephole and see a young couple with luggage standing on the other side.

"Welcome to Edwards Mansion," I say as I open the door. "How may I help you?"

"Hi, we're so sorry to arrive this late," the young woman says apologetically. "We had some car issues and took a wrong turn on the way here."

"It's no problem," I assure them. "Do you have a reservation?"

"Yes, we do," says the man. "Mr. and Mrs. Delany." He looks at the woman and they smile lovingly at each other.

"Ah, yes. You must be the newlyweds," I say as I recall that there's a reservation that was made for the honeymoon suite. Seeing the two of them so happy together, even though their car broke down and it's late, reminds me of what it was like to be that much in love. I miss that feeling. Maybe I *do* want that feeling again—maybe I *am* ready.

I lead the couple inside to the front desk, locking the door behind them. After marking their reservation as checked-in, I hand them their key and give them their room number. "Have a wonderful stay. Let me know if there's anything I can get for you."

"Thank you," says Mr. Delany.

"Have a good night," Mrs. Delany says happily.

"Thank you. You both have a goodnight as well," I say. Once they are on their way upstairs I make my way back to my apartment. As soon as I climb back into bed I fall asleep, dreaming of Gabby.

When I wake up, I feel restless. The fact that I dreamt of Gabby last night is making me anxious because I don't want to let myself get close to anyone ever again. I need to keep things strictly professional with her. But I have a bad feeling that's going to be harder than I think since we're working together every day while she's training.

After taking a shower and getting dressed I head downstairs and make a pot of coffee. I pour myself a cup before walking out onto my patio to sit at the table. The weather is starting to become warmer as summer approaches, and it's a beautiful sunny day today—which makes my mood a little bit better.

After I finish drinking my coffee, I go back inside to grab my keys so I can run a few errands before going to my grandparents' house. I need to pick up a few things for the inn and I promised my grandma I would make chocolate chip cookies for dessert. She loves to cook and bake, but she's always loved my cookies and asks for them whenever she can.

My first stop is at the office supply store to pick up printer paper and more ink. I also grab a package of pens to use until my latest order of monogrammed pens arrives. I bring my items to the checkout where I'm greeted by the cashier who is a friend of my family. "Hi, Brandon! How are you doing today?" she asks.

"Hi, Mrs. Tobin. I'm doing well, thanks. How are you doing?" I ask.

"I'm doing alright. I've just been keeping busy— my house is pretty quiet now with my kids both away at college and my husband is gone on a business trip for a couple of weeks."

"Aww, I bet that's quite an adjustment for you. You're used to having a full house. I remember my mom always telling me that you were busy with sleep-overs for your kids almost every weekend!" I say with a laugh.

"Oh, yes! The kids *always* had friends over," she says fondly. "Anyways—how are things going over at Edwards Mansion?"

I smile warmly at her. "They're going good. We're gearing up for the summer season, and we have a lot of reservations booked starting in a couple of weeks."

"That's great to hear. I'm glad the inn is still such a popular place. It brings in a lot of tourists to our little town, and it's good for our economy. Well—let me ring these items up for you so you can get back to it," she says.

As I complete my purchases I tell Mrs. Tobin it

was great to see her, and head out the door. After climbing into my truck, I make my way over to the grocery store to pick up the ingredients I need for chocolate chip cookies. I quickly run into the grocery store to grab some eggs, butter, and chocolate chips —the few ingredients I don't already have at my apartment—before driving back home.

I park in the garage and carry everything inside. Once I've set the groceries on the counter I preheat the oven for the cookies. I plan on making a double batch so I can bring some to my grandparents' house and put some at the coffee corner in the inn. After double checking my recipe, I mix the ingredients together and scoop the batter onto the cookie sheets. When the oven is preheated I put both of the cookie sheets in and set a timer. A few minutes later the timer dings, and I pull them out. While the cookies are cooling on my counter, I quickly bring the supplies I bought for the inn to my office.

I put the extra batch of cookies in the coffee corner and wave to Chloe at the desk before heading out to my truck. My grandparents' house is about twenty minutes away from the inn, so I text my grandmother that I'll see them soon and pull out onto the main road. As I drive past Gabby's house I can't help but wonder what she is doing today on her day off.

The road that leads to my grandparents' house winds around through thick rows of trees. A small stream runs along the side of the road. As I near the driveway, their large Colonial style house comes into view, situated along the shore of Lake Superior. The house, with its tall white columns framing the front door, looks like it belongs in a painting.

I park in front of the large detached garage at the end of the driveway, climb out of my truck with the cookies, and walk to the door to ring the doorbell. A minute later, a sweet old lady with her grey hair piled on top of her head, and a smile from ear to ear, opens the door. "Hi, Grandma!" I say with a smile as I give her a hug and step inside.

"Hi, dear. You're just in time for a late lunch."

"It smells wonderful in here!"

"I hope so—I've been busy cooking your favorite meal all day. Those wouldn't happen to be your famous chocolate chip cookies, would they?" she asks as I hand her the cookie tin.

"Yes, ma'am."

"Oh splendid," she says happily. "Well, everyone else is out on the patio already. Why don't we go out and join them? It's a beautiful day to be outside after all."

"Who's everyone?" I ask as I raise an eyebrow in confusion. "I thought it was just you, Grandpa, and I."

"Miss Jones stopped over for a visit and brought a new friend. We invited them to stay for lunch. Her friend is new in town and your grandfather and I thought it would be nice for her to be included," she says as she leads me out onto the patio where everyone else is already sitting around a table, laughing and talking.

I smile nervously at my grandma as my heart starts racing. I recognize that voice—I've been trying to get it out of my head all day. Gabby's long brown hair shines in the sun and her eyes widen as she sees me standing there. "Brandon! What are *you* doing here?" she asks in astonishment.

"Hi—Gabby. These are, uh, my grandparents," I say, trying not to stutter. I can't believe she's here.

"Oh! I should have realized who they were with the last name Edwards," she says with a laugh. "I just never put two and two together."

"You two know each other?" my grandpa asks inquisitively.

"Yeah—I hired Gabby not too long ago. She's the new desk clerk at Edwards Mansion."

"So *you're* the new girl I've been hearing so much about. I ran into the O'Learys this morning and they had nothing but nice things to say about you," Grandpa says.

Gabby blushes as she shyly says, "I'm the one. I'm glad the O'Learys had such a great time."

"Well, since you two know each other already, Brandon you can sit next to Gabby. I'll bring the food out," my grandma says happily.

"Hi, Miss Jones," I say as I take a seat next to Gabby. So much for trying to get Gabby out of my head today. I have a feeling this is going to be another long night of tossing and turning.

Chapter Seven

GABBY

I smile at Brandon as he sits down next to me. I feel like such an idiot for not making the connection that Miss Jones's friends are his grandparents. If I had known that ahead of time, I probably would have turned down the invitation to come along and stay for lunch. He sees enough of me at work, he doesn't need to have me hanging around with his family. "I'm sorry," I whisper to him.

"For what?" he asks.

"For intruding on your family time."

"Oh, it's fine. You're not intruding," Brandon says with a smile.

"Of course you're not intruding," Brandon's grandma chimes in. "We invited you! Now, let's eat." She sets a large bowl of spaghetti and a tray of garlic bread in the middle of the table.

"This looks delicious, Mrs. Edwards," I say.

"Oh please! Call me Elizabeth," she says with a laugh as she sits down between her husband and Miss Jones. "Now don't be shy—everyone dig in!"

We all take turns scooping spaghetti onto our plates and pass around the garlic bread. I take a bite and close my eyes as I savor the delicious pasta. "This is amazing!" I say as I open my eyes.

"Thank you," says Elizabeth.

"My wife has always been an excellent cook," says Brandon's grandpa, William, as he looks lovingly at his wife.

"So, Gabby—how are you liking Wilkins Harbor?" asks Elizabeth.

"I love it so far. Everyone here is so welcoming," I say happily.

"And what about working at the inn?" William asks.

"Working at the inn is great, too. It's such a different experience from anything I've ever done before."

"Gabby just accepted a new position at the inn— she's the new pastry chef!" Brandon says excitedly. "Her desserts are out of this world."

"Oh, that's wonderful to hear! How exciting!" Brandon's grandma says.

Miss Jones swallows a bite of garlic bread before saying, "I know I asked the other day, but I have to ask again. How are you liking the house?"

"It's wonderful. I love the view of the lake. It's such a beautiful view to wake up to first thing in the morning. It's so different from my previous home in Arizona."

We continue to have easy conversation as everyone finishes eating. Once we have all cleaned our plates, Brandon pushes back from the table and says, "Let me clean the table for you Grandma and I'll come back with the dessert."

"Thank you dear," says Elizabeth.

"Can I help?" I ask.

Brandon smiles at me. "Sure. That would be great." We carry the plates into the house and rinse them off in the sink. "Thanks for your help, Gabby."

"You're welcome. So—um—I hope this wasn't too uncomfortable for you," I say sheepishly.

"Why would it be uncomfortable?" Brandon asks with a chuckle.

"Oh—I don't know. Because I'm your employee and I just crashed your lunch with your grandparents?" I say. "I know you said it wasn't an intrusion—but I still feel bad."

"Don't worry about it, Gabby. It wasn't uncom-

fortable. I really have had a great afternoon."
Brandon smiles at me as he grabs a tin off of the
counter. "Now, let's go enjoy some dessert. I made it!"

"I love dessert! What did you make?" I ask
curiously.

"Only my world famous chocolate chip cookies!
My grandma loves them," Brandon says with a grin.

"I didn't know you could bake," I say. "You didn't
join us during our baking activity yesterday."

"Nah, I figured I would leave it to you ladies.
Besides, I had to watch the front desk and make sure
all of the other activities ran smoothly. Plus, I didn't
want to show you up in the kitchen," he says with a
wink, looking over his shoulder, as we exit the
kitchen.

Brandon carries the tin back out to the patio and
sets it on the table. "Are those your famous cookies,
Brandon?" asks Miss Jones.

"My world famous cookies?" Brandon chuckles.
"But of course!"

"Your cookies are *fantastic*. I might even eat two!"
Miss Jones says as she reaches for the tin.

"Aww, thanks," says Brandon as he grins at her.

Brandon passes the tin around so we can each
take a cookie. When we're finished with dessert,
Miss Jones and I get ready to leave. "Thank you for

such a lovely afternoon," I say to Elizabeth and William.

"Of course, Gabby. You're welcome back anytime!" says Elizabeth.

I wave goodbye to Brandon and his grandparents. "See you later, Gabby," Brandon says.

"Yeah, see you later," I say. Miss Jones and I walk to her car to make the drive home. "Thank you so much for bringing me along today. And for giving me a ride," I say when we arrive at my house.

"Of course, dear. I'm glad you enjoyed yourself. And, you know, Brandon is such a nice young man. You two would make a cute couple," she says with a wink.

"We're just friends, Miss Jones. I don't think he's interested in dating. Besides—I don't know if *I'm* interested in dating anyone right now either."

"If you say so," she says in a drawn-out tone. "But I still think you two would make a cute couple."

"Have a goodnight, Miss Jones," I say, shaking my head, as I step out of her car. She waves to me with a big grin on her face before driving away.

Pulling my keys out of my purse, I walk up to my front door and unlock it. Once I'm inside I turn on the lights and put my purse down before flopping onto my couch and covering my face. When I agreed to spend the day with Miss Jones, I had no idea that she was going to bring me to Brandon's grandparents' house. Seeing him walk onto that patio this afternoon caught me off guard. I've been attracted to him since the first moment I saw him. Spending time with him on my day off made me want to explore my feelings for him even more, but I need to remember that he's my boss.

Blowing out a breath, I sit up and reach for my cell phone. Opening my favorites list, I choose Alyssa's number and wait for her to answer. "Hey, Gabby," she says as she answers. "What's up?"

"Hey! Are you busy tonight?"

"No. Just planning on watching TV. Why?" she asks.

"I was wondering if you want to come over for a movie night? We haven't had one since I've been here, and I don't have to work tomorrow."

"Sure!" Alyssa says excitedly. "Do you have a specific movie in mind?"

"Not really. Just figured we could browse Netflix and find something," I say.

"Sounds good. I'll pick up some snacks and be over in a bit."

"That would be great, see you soon!" I hang up the phone and change into a pair of comfy pajamas while I wait for Alyssa to arrive. Turning on the television, I open the app for Netflix and try to find something to watch. When my doorbell rings a few minutes later, I open the door to find Alyssa standing there in a pair of flannel pajama pants, holding a bag of snacks.

"Hey! Here's the goodies!" Alyssa says as she hands me the bag of chips, dip, chocolate candy, and sodas.

"Perfect! I was just starting to look for a movie. What kind are you in the mood for?" I ask.

"Hmm—how about a horror movie? It's been awhile since I've watched one," Alyssa says.

"I haven't watched one in a long time either. Let's see what we can find." We sit down on the couch and browse through the titles available. Once we find one that looks good, we select it and push play. We scream and laugh at each other when one of us jumps throughout the movie, just like we used to when we were in college. It brings back great memories of our time together as roommates.

When the movie is over Alyssa turns to me and says, "Now—what was tonight *really* about?"

"What do you mean?" I ask, confused.

"Don't play dumb with me," Alyssa says with a chuckle. "I know you better than that. Sure, you love movies and we always have had movie nights—but something is definitely on your mind tonight."

"I'm fine, really," I say.

"Gabby, come on. What is it?" Alyssa says.

"Alright, alright," I say with a sigh. "I just had an interesting afternoon, that's all. Miss Jones—the lady I bought this house from—invited me to join her to visit some friends. I went along and they invited us to stay for lunch. Well—turns out they were Brandon's grandparents. And Brandon was also there."

"So—what happened?" Alyssa asks.

"Nothing *happened*. But—"

"But what?"

I shake my head and groan. "But I have feelings for Brandon and I shouldn't. He's my boss."

"Oh, Gabby," Alyssa chuckles. "Just because he's your boss doesn't mean you can't like him. But," she says cautiously, "remember what I told you—he hasn't been interested in anyone in a long time."

"I know," I groan. "I'm not holding my breath. But I can't help my feelings. I just need to hide them. Plus, I don't know if *I'm* ready for another relationship. He's just really nice and obviously very attractive."

Alyssa grins at me and chuckles. "Just like old times—movie nights and talking about boy troubles."

I laugh and say, "Some of our best memories

happened on our movie nights." We spend the next half an hour reminiscing about our roommate days before deciding to watch another movie and have a sleepover. Having fun with Alyssa is just what I needed tonight to help me relax and stop thinking about Brandon for awhile.

*A*fter Gabby and Miss Jones leave my grandparents' house, I decide to stay and visit for a bit longer. I haven't seen them in awhile and I want to spend some more time with them. "Thanks again for lunch, Grandma, it was delicious," I say.

"You're welcome. It's been nice spending the afternoon with you, Brandon," Grandma says as she pats my hand.

Grandpa chuckles from his seat next to me. "What's so funny?" I ask.

"Oh, nothing. I was just thinking about the look on your face when you saw Gabby sitting here," he says, still chuckling.

"What look did I have?" I ask curiously. I know

how I was feeling when I saw her. I'm interested to see if I'm able to hide it as well as I think I can.

My grandpa smiles at me knowingly and shakes his head. "I know what you're thinking, son. And no, you can't hide it the way you think you can. You like that girl," he says.

"Well, it doesn't matter," I say. "Nothing is going to happen between us."

"Why not?" asks Grandma.

"Because—I can't. I can't let myself get emotionally attached with anyone again."

"Oh, sweetie," Grandma says sadly, "you can't let the past get in the way of your future. Don't miss out on the chance of being happy and having something wonderful just because of being afraid. I know losing Olivia was hard, but don't let that stop you. Olivia would want you to be happy."

I shake my head. "I'll think about it. But Gabby is just a friend—*and* my employee." I quickly change the topic, steering the conversation away from my love life. "So—are you getting ready for fishing season, Grandpa?" I ask.

"You know I am. Can't wait to get out there and start fishing," he says as he motions towards the water.

"That's good. I'll have to go with you sometime. Either come out here or on one of your fishing trips."

"Sure! Just let me know when you want to tag along," Grandpa says happily.

"Will do," I smile. "How has retirement been otherwise? Still enjoying it?"

"It's been wonderful!" says Grandma. "I have so much more time for my book club and knitting. Plus, your grandpa and I love being able to travel whenever we want without having to worry about how things are going at the inn and if the manager is handling everything alright."

"Plus, I can spend my entire summer fishing if I want to," adds Grandpa.

I laugh. "Sounds like you two are adjusting well to retirement."

"Adjusting? We've been retired for two years!" says Grandpa.

"I know. Just making sure you two weren't bored," I say with a grin. "You were always so busy when you ran Edwards Mansion, I wasn't sure if you would miss it."

"Oh, we miss the people and the inn itself, but we don't miss being so busy."

"Understandable," I say. "I know the people miss you both, too, but at least some of them stay in touch with you."

"Yeah, we still exchange Christmas cards with a few of them. And some of them became good friends of ours. We're actually planning to vacation with one of the couples this summer," Grandma says.

"Really? That's great! That should be nice for you to see them again and interact in a different capacity when you're not hosting them. Where are you all going?" I ask.

"We haven't gotten that far in our planning yet," Grandpa chuckles. "We have a couple of ideas, but the ladies keep going back and forth on which location would have the best food, best sightseeing opportunities, all of that kind of stuff. Bill and I don't care either way where we go—we just want to spend time together as a group."

"Well, I'm sure you'll all figure it out soon." I look at my watch. "Oh, it's pretty late. I didn't notice the time. I'd better get going. Thanks again for a great afternoon. I'm supposed to meet up with Eric soon."

"Okay, you have a good time, dear. And think about what I said," Grandma says as she gives me a hug.

"We love you, Brandon. Come again soon, okay?" says Grandpa.

"Alright. Love you both too," I say as they walk me to the front door. "Have a goodnight." As I climb into my truck, I pull my cell phone out of my pocket and text Eric that I'm on my way. I stop to pick up a six pack of beers before driving over to his house.

When I arrive, I ring the doorbell and wait for him to answer.

The door opens and Eric greets me. "Hey! I see you brought the entry fee—beverages! Come on in."

"You bet I did!" I step inside and kick off my shoes before bringing the beers into the kitchen and putting them in his refrigerator. Grabbing two of them, I hand one to Eric and open the other for myself.

"How was lunch with your grandparents? How are they doing these days?" Eric asks.

"They're both doing good. Grandpa is getting excited for fishing season and I think Grandma is just enjoying not having to work. They said they're planning a vacation with some former guests that they became good friends with," I say as I take a long drink of my beer.

Eric raises a brow. "Thirsty, Brandon?"

Narrowing my eyes at him, I say, "Yeah, I am actually."

Eric chuckles. "So—if everything is great with your grandparents, what happened at lunch?"

"Nothing happened at lunch," I answer defensively as I take another long pull and finish my beer.

"If nothing happened, why have you finished off your beer so quickly? As long as I've known you, you don't drink much. You usually *nurse* your beers."

Ignoring Eric, I grab another beer from the fridge and head into the living room to sit on the couch. "Are we going to play video games or what? I thought that's why I came over."

"Alright, alright," Eric says as he takes a seat on the other end of the couch. "But I'm going to get it out of you before you leave tonight." Eric turns on the PlayStation and flips on Madden NFL. We play against each other for a few minutes before he puts the controller down on the coffee table. "Dude, you suck tonight! Beating you isn't even challenging! It's twenty-one to zero and it's only the end of the first quarter."

"Ugh," I say as I scrub my hand over my face. Taking a deep breath and leaning back I finally mutter, "Gabby was at my grandparents today."

Eric stops mid-sip of his beer. "Gabby—what?"

"She was at my grandparents for lunch. She came with Miss Jones and we ended up sitting next to each other. And after she left, my grandpa called me out on liking her."

"Oh," Eric says as understanding dawns on him. "And now you're terrified because you don't want to admit your feelings?"

"I don't want to *have* feelings," I correct him.

"Yeah, well, you can't help that," he says. "What are you going to do?"

"I'm not going to *do* anything. I'm going to keep training her at work and once she's ready to be on her own, I'll only see her when I absolutely have to."

"Brandon—"

"Save it. My grandma already gave me the speech about not missing out on the opportunity just because I'm scared. I don't need to hear it again," I say as I finish beer number two.

"Alright, alright. Want another beer?" Eric asks, knowing that I don't want to discuss it any further.

"Sure. Thanks."

Eric goes into the kitchen and comes back with a beer for each of us and a bowl of popcorn. "Now, get your head in the game. It's going to be boring if you don't start giving me some competition!"

I force myself to stop thinking about Gabby—and everything I discussed with my grandparents and Eric —and focus on the game in front of me. Eric and I spend the rest of the night battling against each other in our favorite video game and by the time we call it a night, I'm relaxed and feeling better. Now if only I can learn how to suppress my feelings *all* of the time, especially when I'm around Gabby, I'll get through working with her just fine.

Chapter Nine

GABBY

I've been working at Edwards Mansion for a couple of weeks now. Ever since that day at Brandon's grandparents' house he's been acting —different. We still work most of the shifts together, but he rarely talks about anything besides work-related topics. I need to keep reminding myself that he's my boss and this is the way it should be. I can't let my feelings get hurt by it.

It's almost our busy season and although there won't be any night shifts scheduled just yet, Brandon has me working one so that I can see what it'll be like. He'll be here with me since I've never worked a night shift before, but I'm feeling more comfortable with everything since I've been training with him for a while. The doors to the inn are already locked for the night, and the doorbell can be heard through a portable monitor, so there is no reason for us to stay at the desk the whole time.

"Will you be alright on your own for a little bit if I go handle some paperwork in my office?" Brandon asks.

"Sure! I'll be fine."

"Okay. I'll be back," he says as he walks towards his office.

After about a half an hour sitting at the desk on my own, I hear music coming from the music room. The room is soundproofed as long as the door is closed, but since I can hear the music I'm guessing whoever it is has the door propped open a bit. I grab the monitor for the doorbell and wander down the hall to see who's playing at this hour.

Peeking into the room, I see Brandon sitting at the piano. I smile to myself and quietly step inside. The piano sings, softly at first, then louder as the music grows with such intensity and emotion. The warm glow of the fireplace seems to dance to the tune as it flicks and races up the wall. He looks up and stops playing when he notices me standing near the doorway. "No, please don't stop," I beg. "That sounded beautiful."

Brandon smiles and nods before he starts playing again without speaking a word. The sound fills the room as he gracefully plays the piano with what seems to be little effort. He looks so peaceful and calm, but with a sadness in his face and eyes that I haven't seen before. As the song ends Brandon slowly looks up at me. "Gabby, come sit by me," he says as he pats the bench beside him. "Sorry—I know I said I'd be right back to the desk, but after the paperwork I just wandered over here. "

It's nice to have him interact with me this way again and I can't help the feeling of happiness that rushes through me. I walk over and sit on the bench next to him. "It's alright. I wondered where you'd disappeared to. When was the last time you played?" I ask. "The first day I started here, when you showed me the music room, you mentioned that you hadn't played in a long time."

Brandon lowers his head, and a single tear runs down his cheek. "The last time I played was the night Olivia died. I haven't played since then—until tonight."

"Oh—who was Olivia?" I ask somberly, knowing that this person must have meant a great deal to him.

"She was my fiancée."

"I'm so sorry," I say as my heart breaks for him. "What happened, if you don't mind my asking?"

Brandon shakes his head. "I don't mind. Two years ago, she was in a car accident. It was the middle of winter and she was on her way here to meet me for dinner. She hit a patch of black ice, lost control of the vehicle, and flipped her car. It rolled a few times before slamming into a tree." He chokes on a sob with his next words. "She died before she even reached the hospital." His eyes fill with tears again.

Without even thinking about it, I reach out and pull him into a hug. He hesitates for only a moment before wrapping his arms around me and hugging me back. We hold each other for a few minutes before finally pulling apart. Brandon clears his throat and says, "So—do you want to learn how to play? I'll teach you. No charge." He gives me a half smile.

"Really?" I ask excitedly.

"Sure," he says as he wipes his face.

Brandon takes my hand and helps me place my fingers on the correct keys before guiding me through a simple C major scale a few times. "Good," he says. "Now let's add your left hand. Remember to keep your hands relaxed." After practicing a few more times with both hands, I turn and smile at Brandon.

"Thanks for teaching me," I say, shyly.

"You're welcome. And I wanted to say that I'm sorry if I've been a little cold lately. I've just been —distracted."

"It's alright. You're my boss—I understand that. There's no need to apologize," I say.

Brandon's quiet for a minute before he says,

"Okay. Let's get back to practicing." He motions to the piano. "Try it on your own this time."

I place my fingers on the keys and do my best to play the notes that he taught me. Feeling his body so close to mine as he reaches to reposition my hands makes heat rush through me and I can feel myself blushing. Clearing my throat I softly ask, "How was that?"

"Better," he says with a smile. "You can come in here anytime to practice. Maybe I can give you a few more lessons sometime."

"That would be nice." As Brandon's leg brushes up against mine, it feels like every one of my nerve endings are firing. My stomach is full of butterflies and my palms are starting to sweat. I need to get out of here before I do something stupid. "I'm—ah—going to make sure everything is still alright at the front desk. You know, make sure no guests have wandered downstairs needing something. Excuse me." I quickly stand up from the piano bench and rush out of the room, leaving Brandon sitting alone.

I feel terrible for running out on him as I walk into the bathroom. I make my way to the sink and turn on the cold water faucet. Dipping my hands under the freezing liquid, I splash it on my face to rein my feelings back under control. "Get a grip, Gabby. He just got done telling you about losing his fiancée. You can't get involved with him," I tell myself as I look at my reflection in the mirror. Turning off the water, I grab a piece of paper towel to dry my face and take a deep breath before leaving the bathroom and walking out to the front desk.

As expected, everything is quiet and no one else is around. I pull out the chair behind the desk and sit down. Closing my eyes, I fold my arms on the desktop and rest my head on top of them. This is going to be a long night if I'm going to be around Brandon. I've got to try my best to avoid him for the rest of our shift.

By the time Chloe arrives for the morning shift, I'm anxious to head home. I wasn't able to avoid Brandon for my whole shift, but at least I was able to keep my feelings under control for the most part. But now I need to go home and take a cold shower. "Hi, Gabby," Chloe says cheerfully as she walks behind the desk to put her belongings in the closet.

"Hi, Chloe!" I say as I quickly grab my things and prepare to leave.

"How did you like the night shift?" Chloe asks.

"It was fine. Uneventful," I say. "Sorry I can't stay to chat longer, but I've got somewhere I need to be."

I wave to her and start to walk out the door, but Brandon stops me.

"Hey, Gabby! Wait up!" he says as he catches up to me. "Is everything alright? You've been acting a little strange over the last couple of hours," he says with concern.

"Yeah, I'm fine. Sorry—just a little tired I guess."

He doesn't look like he entirely believes me, but nods as he says, "Alright. Have a good day, Gabby. I'll see you on Friday then."

"See you on Friday," I say as I turn to walk towards the parking lot. Thoughts of Brandon running to catch up with me and holding me in his arms run through my head. Just as quickly as they came, I push those thoughts back out. I quickly get into my car and drive home—without a single glance towards the inn.

When I arrive home a little while later, I park in my driveway and make my way inside. After dropping my purse on the floor in my bedroom I go into the bathroom to turn on the shower. I strip off my clothes and step under the spray of hot water. As the water beats down on me and steam fills the room, my emotions run wild in my head.

After rinsing off and toweling dry, I put on my pajamas and crawl into bed. As weird as it will seem sleeping during the day, I'm completely exhausted after my shift. The last twelve hours have been a rollercoaster of emotions, and have left me mentally exhausted too. Resting my head on my fluffy pillow and wrapping up in the soft blankets, I feel relaxed and quickly drift off to sleep.

Gabby arrives at the inn for her shift early on Friday morning. "Good morning, Brandon," she says as she puts her coat and purse in the closet behind the desk. She seems to be back to her normal, cheery self—no longer acting the way she was a couple of days ago.

"Good morning. You look nice today," I say as I take in her floral dress with leggings.

"Thank you," she says cheerfully. "I'm going out after work and didn't know if I'd have time to go home to change."

"Where are you going?" I ask conversationally.

"I'm going to the *Countdown to Summer Music Festival*. Alyssa and I ran into Eric yesterday and he invited us to join him.

I clench my jaw at the thought of Gabby going

out with another guy. Even if it *is* Eric and Alyssa will be there too. Ever since that night in the music room, when she wrapped me in a hug, I can't get the thought of her out of my head. The feel of her body so close to mine, the sweet scent of her hair—like fresh raspberries.

Knowing that Gabby is going to the festival—and not wanting her to go with Eric—makes my decision of whether or not I want to go an easy one. "So—I planned on heading over there after work, too. Would you—maybe—want to drive over there together? We can meet Eric and Alyssa there," I say a little awkwardly.

Gabby smiles at me. "Sure, that would be great."

"Perfect. Um—can you handle the desk for a minute while I run to my office?"

"Sure, no problem."

Walking back to my office, I curse under my breath. I grab my cell phone off my desk where I left it this morning and open a text to Eric.

Me: You asked Gabby to the festival tonight?!

Eric: I did. And Alyssa.

Eric: Since you said you weren't interested, I thought maybe I should go out with the new girl in town. ;) Is that a problem?

Me: Yes...no...I don't know! Ugh. To be honest it kind of pissed me off when I found out she was going with you—even if it was supposed to be with Alyssa.

Eric: Ha! You're jealous!

Me: Yes, I am actually. And I'm not sure how I feel about that. It's been so long since I've felt anything for a woman.

Eric: It's about time, man. You just needed a little push.

Me: You asked her on purpose to piss me off, didn't you?

Eric: Of course I did. I figured you wouldn't ask on your own. After our conversation that night you came over to play video games....you were determined to NOT feel anything. But I know you better than that. I could see how much you like her.

Me: Well...thanks for pushing me then I guess.

Eric: You're welcome.

Me: Guess that means we'll be on a double date. You and Alyssa with Gabby and I.

Eric: Not a date...Alyssa and I are just friends.

Me: If you say so. I'll see you later. I have to get back to work.

Eric: Alright. See you tonight.

I walk back out to the desk with a new feeling of happiness. "Sorry that took so long," I say.

"That's alright," Gabby says with a smile. "Mr. and

Mrs. Jameson checked out and wanted me to tell you that they will be back in the fall per usual to take the color tour."

"Ah, yes. They always come here at least twice a year, sometimes more."

"They seemed like such a nice older couple."

"They are. They're friends with my grandparents so I've seen a lot of them," I say.

"That's great," says Gabby.

"Yeah, it's always nice when the regular guests become personal friends."

Gabby smiles at me before she says, "I finished reconciling all of the receipts and money from yesterday." She hands me the cash bag and a stack of credit card receipts. "I also made sure that housekeeping is aware of all of the rooms that are ready to be cleaned."

"Perfect! Sounds like you're doing well on your own. Are you ready to start working by yourself next shift?" I ask. She looks a little disappointed at this idea so I quickly add, "I'll still be around the building of course—you know, if you need anything."

Perking up, Gabby says, "Yeah, I think I can handle it on my own next shift. But I *am* glad that you'll be around."

Smiling at Gabby I say, "Alright. I'll adjust the

schedule for next week. But—in the meantime, let's get through this shift."

We decide to take a walk through the common areas to see if any of the guests need anything. There's a family in the library with two young children looking for books. "Hi," Gabby whispers. "Is there anything we can help you find?"

"We were trying to find something that would be a good bedtime story. I need to get these two down for a nap at some point this afternoon and I want to be prepared," the mother says as she juggles one of her toddlers on her hip while her husband reaches for the other as he's about to climb on a bookshelf.

Gabby smiles and kneels down to talk to the boy now standing next to his father. "Do you like *Winnie the Pooh?*" The boy shyly nods his head yes as he clings to his father's leg. "What about your sister? Does she like *Winnie the Pooh?*" Gabby asks.

"She likes Tigger!" says the little boy.

"I think you might be in luck, then, because I think I saw *both* of them in a book over there," she says as she points to a small corner shelf.

"Yay!" says the little boy excitedly.

"Thank you," says the mother as Gabby stands to lead them to the children's books. I smile as I take in the sight of Gabby interacting with them. She's good with children and I can't help but feel like maybe *someday* she will make a good mother to *my* children. Which is a ridiculous thought because I don't even want a relationship at the moment, let alone kids. But ever since the day Gabby first came to Edwards Mansion, I've been feeling things that I haven't felt in forever, so I may as well add this to the list.

After the family finds the book and heads back to their room, I tell Gabby, "You're really good with kids, you know that?"

"Thanks. I have lots of cousins and I babysat a lot in high school," she says.

We walk out into the hallway and make our way to the sunroom to see if anything else needs to be done. No one else is in any of the common areas, so we head back to the front desk. "It's such a nice day today, it looks like everyone is enjoying the outdoors," I say.

"It *is* a nice day today. I'm glad it's finally warming up. I'm not a huge fan of cold weather."

"Ha!" I laugh. "You moved *here* and you're not a fan of cold weather? You *do* know what the winters are like, right?"

Gabby grins at me. "I've never actually been here for a winter, but Alyssa has told me about them. I'm hoping I'll learn to love cold weather."

"Well thankfully you've got a summer to enjoy

first. There's at least a couple of months before the snow falls," I tease.

"A couple of months? But—but summer is just starting," Gabby sputters.

"Don't worry," I say with a smile. "You'll get used to how much snow we receive. Eventually."

"Gee, thanks," she says sarcastically.

Back at the desk, Gabby and I handle a few guests checking in and out before spending the next few hours discussing what we're looking forward to most over the summer. We wait for Chloe to arrive for the afternoon shift and as soon as she does, Gabby and I are ready to head to the music festival. Tonight could be really good for me. I'm looking forward to spending some time with her outside of work.

Chapter Eleven

GABBY

I wave to Chloe as she arrives for her shift. "Hey, Chloe!"

"Hey, Gabby! How has your day been?" Chloe asks.

"It's been great. It's been pretty slow, just a few check-outs and check-ins like usual," I say as I grab my purse and jacket out of the closet.

"Hi, Chloe," Brandon says. "Gabby, I need to run to my place really quick before we head to the festival. Do you want to come with me?"

"Sure." I follow Brandon to the other side of the inn to his apartment. Brandon unlocks his door and motions for me to step inside first. He follows me in and shuts the door behind him. Looking around, Brandon's home has the same historical feel as the rest of Edwards Mansion. But it has more modern touches. "You're home is beautiful, Brandon."

"Thank you. My grandparents lived here until they retired. As you know, they moved out and bought that Colonial style cottage on the lake. My grandfather loves it—he can walk out his front door and go fishing every morning in the summer. When I moved in here, I updated it so that it was more my style."

"You kept some historical pieces though I see," I say with a smile.

Brandon chuckles. "Of course I did. I had to keep my grandmother happy." We walk into the living room and Brandon motions to the couch. "Go ahead and make yourself comfortable. I'm going to run upstairs to change. I'll be right back."

"Okay," I say as I sit down. I pull out my cell phone as I wait for Brandon to come back downstairs. I have a text message from Alyssa.

Alyssa: Hey, Gabby. I talked to Eric and he said there was a change of plans. Are you not coming?
Me: Hey! Sorry for the delay...I was working. Yes, I'm still coming. But Brandon asked me to go with him, so I'm coming with him and I'll see you there.
Alyssa: Brandon asked you?! As in Brandon Edwards?

I chuckle to myself as I respond.

Me: Yes, Brandon Edwards. Don't be so surprised...he's probably just being nice. He probably thought he would give me a ride since we are both planning on going anyways.
Alyssa: Even if it is just as friends, Brandon Edwards hasn't even spent time with women who are friends in years.
Me: Well, whatever he was thinking when he asked me, doesn't really matter. I'm coming with him and I'll see you there.
Alyssa: See you soon!

"Alright. I'm ready to go if you are," Brandon says as he comes back down the stairs.

Slipping my phone back into my purse, I smile up at Brandon. "Yeah, I'm ready."

He leads me through a door that opens directly to the outside instead of having to go back through the inn. We make our way to his truck, which is parked inside a garage at the back of the property.

After we climb into his truck, Brandon backs out and turns onto the main road. "So, how are you liking Wilkins Harbor so far?" he asks.

"I love it! It's so different from Arizona."

"I bet it is."

"The weather here is colder than I'm used to, but I love the small town life so far. Granted I haven't been here very long, but from what I've seen everyone is so friendly."

"Yeah, living in a small town definitely has it's perks," Brandon says.

In only a few minutes we pull into the parking lot at the park where the festival is being held. The park is already full of people crowded around listening to the music, drinking beer, and eating food from the local vendors who have their food carts set up. The smell of fried food and sweet treats wafts through the air, making my mouth water, as we climb out of the truck and make our way into the crowd to find Alyssa and Eric.

"Do you see them anywhere?" Brandon asks as he scans the crowd.

"No, I don't," I say shaking my head.

We walk over towards the tent that's set up in front of the stage where the bands are performing. "Gabby! Over here!" I hear Alyssa shout. Scanning the crowd under the tent, I see Alyssa and Eric sitting at a table in the middle.

"There they are," I say to Brandon as I point in the direction of their table. We both walk over to join them. "Hey!" I say to both of them as Brandon and I sit down. "How's the music?"

"Good so far," Eric says. "Keweenaw Country doesn't play for a while still, though."

"That's alright. Glad we made it with plenty of time before they play," Brandon says. He turns to me and says, "I'm going to grab a beer; do you want anything?"

"I'll have a beer too, please. Whatever you're having," I smile.

"Do you two want anything?" he asks Alyssa and Eric.

"Yeah, I'll come with you," Eric says. "You want another one?" he asks Alyssa.

"Yes, please."

Brandon and Eric head off in the direction of the drink vendor while Alyssa and I talk and save our table. "Have you and Eric been here long?" I ask.

"Not too long, but we did come a little bit earlier than we had originally planned since you decided to come with Brandon," Alyssa says.

I look down to try to hide my blush. "Yeah—I felt kind of bad for backing out of coming with you guys since Eric invited both of us, but when Brandon asked me I couldn't say no."

"I bet you couldn't," Alyssa teases.

"Like I told you earlier, I don't think it means anything. We're just friends."

"Whatever you say," Alyssa says as the guys return with our drinks.

"What are you ladies talking about?" Eric asks.

"Nothing," I say quickly while Alyssa gives him a mischievous smile.

Brandon and Eric sit down as the band finishes and Keweenaw Country prepares to take the stage. The four of us enjoy our beers as we listen to the music and joke around with each other. The band finishes the song they were playing and starts another.

"Aww—I love this song," Alyssa says as the soft, slow tune begins. "Come on, let's dance." She pulls Eric by the hand to the dance floor.

Brandon and I smile at each other as we watch them go. After a minute Brandon nods his head towards the dance floor. "Want to dance?" he asks.

"Sure," I say as we stand.

We walk to the middle of the floor and find a spot next to Alyssa and Eric. Brandon places his hands on my hips and pulls me close. It's like a jolt of electricity shooting through me at his touch. The night we hugged in the music room I wasn't thinking about my feelings because of the circumstances that led to that hug, but now I can't help it—I have butterflies at the feeling of Brandon's hands on me. Sucking in a deep breath, I wrap my arms around Brandon's neck and we start to sway slowly to the music.

I look up into Brandon's eyes as he smiles down at me. Brandon's hand glides up my side to cup the back of my neck as he leans down to kiss me. It's a slow, passionate kiss that leaves us both breathless when we pull apart.

Brandon closes his eyes and lets go of me. "I'm sorry. I—I shouldn't have done that. Excuse me for a minute." He walks briskly off the dance floor and towards the parking lot.

Alyssa and Eric come up beside me. "What happened?" asks Alyssa.

"I don't know," I say, shaking my head.

"I'll go talk to him," Eric says as he hurries after Brandon.

"Are you okay, Gabby?" Alyssa asks.

"Uh—yeah, I'm fine I guess. I'm just not sure what happened. We were dancing—and then he kissed me and—"

"And then he freaked out and ran off," Alyssa finishes for me.

"Yeah," I say sadly.

"Oh, Gabby. I'm sorry. I'm sure he just needs a minute. This is all new for him. He hasn't been on a date in quite a while."

"Yeah, I know. I just don't want things to get awkward between us at work." Alyssa gives me a hug before we make our way back to our table. All I can do now is wait to see if Brandon comes back with Eric or not.

Chapter Twelve

BRANDON

*a*s I pace back and forth in the parking lot, I see Eric walking towards me. "Hey. You alright? What happened?" he asks.

I rub my face with my hand as I stop pacing. "I kissed her. I kissed Gabby and then I panicked," I say miserably. "I just don't know if I'm ready for another relationship."

Eric pats me on the shoulder. "It's alright to be scared, Brandon. But don't miss out on your chance with Gabby because of it. Olivia wouldn't want you to be alone. She would want you to be happy."

I take a deep, shuddery breath and blow it out. "Yeah, I know she would want me to be happy. I'm just afraid I'm going to fall in love with her and— what if I lose her too?"

"But what if you fall in love with her and *don't* lose

her?" Eric asks. "Are you going to be able to live with the *what ifs* if you don't take a chance?"

I growl in frustration before answering. "No. No, I don't think I'd be able to live with the what ifs."

"So—what are you going to do?" Eric asks.

"I'm going to walk my ass back in there and apologize to Gabby for running off."

"Good," Eric says with a smile.

We walk back into the festival and find Gabby and Alyssa talking at our table. "Hey, Gabby," I say as I catch her gaze. "Can we talk for a minute? Please?"

"Sure," Gabby says as she stands up from the table.

I lead her to the edge of the park, away from the music where it's quieter. Turning to face her I say, "Gabby, I'm sorry."

"It's alright, Brandon. I understand," she says quietly. "You just got caught up in the moment."

"No," I say shaking my head. "I mean, I'm sorry for freaking out on you. I kissed you and the way it made me feel—scared me. I haven't felt this way about anyone in a long time." I take her hands in mine. "Please forgive me for running off on you."

Gabby smiles at me. "Of course I forgive you. And I understand why you're scared. We don't need to rush into anything."

I lean my forehead against Gabby's. "We'll take it

slow, then." I bring my lips to hers and kiss her. This time when we pull apart I smile at her. "I really like you Gabby."

"I like you too, Brandon."

Taking her hand in mine, I lead her back towards the music. When we arrive at our table we see that Alyssa and Eric are dancing again. The song finishes and they walk over to join us where we're sitting. Eric smiles at me and I see Alyssa's eyes go wide when they see my hand clasped around Gabby's.

"You guys look like you're having fun," Gabby says.

"Yeah! The music is really great!" Alyssa says happily. "Are you two planning on sticking around a little longer?"

I look at Gabby who nods her head. "Sure, we'll stick around for a bit," I say.

"Good! I'm going to steal Gabby for a few minutes then," Alyssa says.

I watch with a grin as she pulls Gabby out to dance. When I turn my attention back to the table, Eric is smirking at me. "Don't look at me like that," I chuckle.

"I can't help it," Eric says. "I knew if I gave you a push, you would end up with her."

"Not so fast. Who knows if we'll end up together *forever*. We decided to take things slow. But thanks for that push. I guess I have been pretty closed off these last couple of years."

"Yeah, you have been. I'm just glad you're finally willing to put yourself out there again," he says.

The band announces that they'll be performing the final song of the night. Eric and I walk to the dance floor to join Alyssa and Gabby for one last dance. We all laugh and dance together, enjoying the performance.

When the music is finished, we all walk to the parking lot together before Gabby and I say goodbye to Eric and Alyssa. I open the door for Gabby and she climbs into my truck. As we drive back to Edwards Mansion, I ask Gabby, "So—what did you think about your first music festival in the Keweenaw?"

"I loved it!" Gabby says cheerfully. "The music was really good and the dancing was a lot of fun. I didn't realize there were so many people in this town though!" she says with a laugh.

I chuckle. "Yeah, the festival tends to bring the whole town out. Plus all of the neighboring towns too."

Gabby is quiet for a few minutes before saying, "I had a great time tonight, Brandon."

"So did I, Gabby." I reach across the seat to hold her hand. As we pull into the parking lot of the inn I tell her, "I'm going to park in my garage and I'll walk you back to your car, if you don't mind."

"I don't mind," she smiles. "But you really don't need to walk me out to my car. I'll be fine."

"I know you would be—but I would like to." I pull into my garage and turn the truck off before going around to open the door for Gabby. "Would you rather go through the inn or walk around the grounds to the parking lot?" I ask.

"It's such a nice night. Let's walk the grounds."

We walk hand in hand along the walking path which is lit by a string of Edison light bulbs. The sound of flowing water from the creek breaks the silence of the night. A warm breeze gently blows through Gabby's hair, and it tickles my arm. We walk together in a comfortable silence, enjoying the beauty around us.

When we arrive at Gabby's car, I wrap my arms around her and pull her close. "Thank you," I say.

"For what?" she asks as she furrows her brow, confused.

"For coming with me to the festival. For forgiving me for freaking out on you. For giving me a chance even though I'm a broken man."

"Brandon, you're not broken. Healing from a broken heart, maybe, but I think you still have a lot of love to give. I understand that a part of you will always love Olivia, but that's okay. You set the pace with how fast we take our relationship. I'm not going anywhere."

I smile at Gabby's kind words and lean down to give her a kiss. "Thanks. I appreciate that. I'll call you tomorrow?"

"Sounds good. Have a goodnight, Brandon."

"You, too. Drive home safe, okay?"

"I promise I will. I'll even text you when I get there if you want." Gabby says.

"That would be nice," I say.

Gabby climbs into her SUV and waves as she pulls out of the parking lot. I watch as she drives away. And I realize I'm happy for the first time in a really long time.

I wake up to the sound of birds chirping and sunlight streaming in through my window. Thoughts of last night race through my head, and I sigh happily at the memory of Brandon's soft kiss, his lips against mine. Thinking of what it felt like to be in his arms makes me smile.

My thoughts are interrupted by a vibrating rumble on the table next to me. I reach over and grab my cell phone to see that it's Brandon calling me. "Hey, Gabby," he says when I answer.

"Hey," I say. "How are you this morning?"

"I'm good. I was wondering—would you like to do something with me today?" he asks.

"Sure! What did you have in mind?"

"I was thinking we could do a little sightseeing, maybe have a picnic."

"That sounds great!" I say excitedly. "Any particular sights you had in mind?"

"I was thinking we could go explore Fort Keweenaw, and go to the top of Copper Mountain. The view is spectacular from up there," Brandon says.

"Awesome! I've heard that both are a must see, and I've wanted to go to both of those places, but I haven't had the chance yet."

"Perfect! I'll pack the picnic lunch and pick you up in half an hour? Could you be ready by then?"

"Yep, sounds good," I say. "See you soon." Hanging up the phone, I choose some clothes from my closet before heading into the bathroom to take a quick shower. By the time Brandon rings my doorbell thirty minutes later, I'm all ready to go. "Hi!" I say as I open the door.

"You ready?" Brandon asks with a smile.

"Yep! All set!" I grab my purse and lock the door behind me as Brandon leads me out to his truck. He opens the door for me and lets me climb in before walking around to his side. He's such a gentleman. I'm not used to that—Tim was the complete opposite.

When he climbs in Brandon asks, "Where would you like to go first? Fort Keweenaw or Copper Mountain?"

"Hmm—let's go to the fort first," I say.

"Sounds good." Brandon pulls out of the driveway and heads towards Fort Keweenaw. "Have you heard any of the history about the fort?"

"Not really," I say. "Alyssa mentioned it to me when I was making a list of places I want to check out, but she didn't really tell me anything about it."

"Well, you can read more about it when we get there, but basically it was an active Army fort in the mid 1800s, and now it's a historical state park. You can tour the museum, and there are also camping sites that you can use, which is a ton of fun in the summer."

"I'm excited to see it," I say as we pull into the parking lot.

We climb out of the truck and Brandon takes my hand as we walk down the path that leads to Fort Keweenaw. The path brings us to a large open field surrounded by buildings. In the middle of the field is a large flag pole next to an old cannon which is facing a small lake.

As we step into the first building, I see that it's one of several quarters made for married enlisted men and their families. Behind the glass windows, I can see the items they would have had, such as furniture, clothing, books, and children's toys.

In another building there are rooms and items that would have been used by military officers.

Uniforms lie neatly on the beds, and official documents and weapons are spread out on the tables.

In the infirmary building there is a row of beds with tables and medicines, as well as a doctor's surgical items. As we walk through the other buildings—housing the mess halls, blacksmith's shop, and barracks to name a few places—it's fascinating to see all of the artifacts from the 1800s.

When we have finished looking in each of the buildings we take a quick walk through the gift shop that was built for the museum, and I purchase a magnet for my refrigerator. "That was really cool. Thanks for bringing me here," I say.

"Of course," says Brandon. "Now how about we head up to Copper Mountain, and then we can go to a great spot I know for our picnic?"

"Sounds like a plan," I say with a smile.

We drive to the top of Copper Mountain, which is more like a big hill compared to the mountains I've seen before, and park the truck. The parking lot is full of cars, and there are people wandering around taking photos and exploring.

After climbing out, we walk towards the viewing deck on the edge which overlooks the entire town. I can see the rows of houses and restaurants down below, and Lake Superior—with water extending beyond the horizon—filled with boats of all sizes.

There are small fishing boats, as well as the large freighter ships that pass through here. In the distance is a beautiful red and white lighthouse. I put my hand up to shade my eyes from the bright sunlight as I take in the beautiful view.

"If you look over there," Brandon says, pointing, "you can see the top of Edwards Mansion."

"Wow! This view really is amazing," I say in awe.

Brandon wraps his arms around me as we take in the view for a few more minutes. I lean back against him, enjoying the feeling of being in his arms. Last night after he kissed me, it's been all I've been able to think about. I wasn't sure if he would even go through with trying to start a relationship with me after he got so freaked out last night—even if we did end the night saying we were going to take it slow. I thought maybe he would chicken out. But I was happy this morning when he called, and being here in his arms is the best feeling ever.

We walk back to the truck and make the drive down the mountain. "So—where is this perfect picnic spot of yours?" I ask.

"You'll see," says Brandon with a grin. "It's a surprise."

We drive a few miles down the road until we come to a parking lot with stairs leading down the side of a hill. Brandon grabs the picnic basket and a blanket and leads me down the steps onto a sandy beach along Lake Superior. The tiny waves gently lap against the shore, and I can see small children happily playing in the water a little farther down the beach. "You're right," I say. "This *is* perfect!"

We walk along the sand until we get to a flat spot shaded by trees. Brandon spreads out the blanket and we sit down. "Are you ready for lunch?" he asks.

"Sure. What did you bring?"

"Food." Brandon chuckles and grins.

"Ha, ha. Very funny. I meant what *kind* of food?" I ask with a laugh.

"Why didn't you say so?" he jokes. "In that case— let's look." Opening the basket, he pulls out sand-wiches, fruit, and bottles of water. There are even a couple of chocolate chip cookies.

"This looks great, Brandon."

He smiles at me and says, "Go ahead and dig in."

We look out over the water, watching the large freighters float by, as we eat our lunch. "Thanks for showing me all of these places. The fort was really neat—I've never seen anything like that before—and the view from the top of Copper Mountain was spec-tacular. I've had a wonderful day," I say.

Brandon leans over and tucks a piece of hair behind my ear. Looking into my eyes he says, "I've had a wonderful day so far too, Gabby." He lowers his head until his lips softly touch mine. He kisses me, gently at first, then slowly he parts my lips with his tongue. My body heats up as his hand traces up and down my arm. When we pull apart, I'm left breathless.

I smile as I look deep into his eyes. He takes my hand in his before asking, "Was that okay? Not too much?"

Shaking my head, "No, it's not too much."

"Okay good. I haven't done this in a while, and I'm a little rusty," Brandon says with a chuckle.

"Well, it was perfect. The whole day has been," I say. Brandon wraps an arm around me and we sit together, enjoying each other's company in silence, while we watch the waves lap against the shore.

The weather starts to turn chillier as the sun starts to sink lower in the sky and I shiver. "Are you cold?" Brandon asks.

"A little."

"Alright. Let's get you home then," he says as he kisses the top of my head. We gather up our picnic basket and the blanket and climb the stairs to the parking lot. After putting them into the truck, we get in and make the drive back to my house. Brandon pulls into my driveway and puts the truck in park.

"Thanks for the wonderful day, Brandon," I say.

"I'm glad I could make it special," he says. He

turns the engine off and walks around to my side of the truck to open the door before walking me inside. Giving me a kiss he says, "Have a goodnight Gabby."

"You too." I lock the door behind Brandon and watch through the window as he pulls out of the driveway. As I walk to my bedroom to change into my pajamas, I can't help but think that I'm falling in love with Brandon.

Chapter Fourteen

BRANDON

The last couple of days with Gabby have felt fantastic. I don't even remember the last time I felt this happy. I still want to take things slow though, because I'm terrified to fall in love again. Terrified of getting my heart broken. When I lost Olivia, it felt like my heart was ripped out of my chest and shattered.

I still remember that night so clearly—I was in my apartment waiting for her to arrive. When the doorbell rang and I saw Eric standing there in his uniform with a sad expression on his face, I knew something had happened. I was instantly filled with panic and a fear like nothing I've ever experienced before. The moment he told me what had happened, it was like my entire world was crashing down around me. I'm not sure my heart can handle something like that again, but being with Gabby makes me feel whole again so I'm willing to see where things go.

Gabby and I both have the day off today so we made plans this afternoon to go for a walk along the lakeshore, maybe take a sightseeing cruise. First I'm meeting Eric for breakfast though. After showering and dressing, I make the short drive to Murphy's Cafe, the local diner that we planned to meet at. When I walk in, the smell of bacon and freshly baked pastries hits my nose. Customers chatter noisily as they eat their breakfasts. I tell the hostess I'm meeting someone, and scan the room to find Eric seated at a booth by the window.

I make my way over and take a seat across from him. "Good morning," I say.

"Morning," Eric says as he takes a sip of coffee.

"You didn't order me a cup?" I tease.

"Sorry, man. I didn't want yours to get cold, but I needed some caffeine."

"Rough night?" I ask.

"Yeah. Big accident on the edge of town last night. I had to help with the wreckage cleanup— didn't get home until late."

"That sucks," I say understandingly. "I definitely don't envy you. I don't think I could handle dealing with accidents and fires."

"Someone has to do it," Eric says.

"Hi, guys. What can I get for you?" the waitress asks as she walks over to take our orders.

"I'll have the daily special, please. Eggs over easy, bacon, and white toast, with a coffee," I say.

She turns to Eric. "Alright, and for you?"

"I'll have the same please, but make my eggs scrambled."

"You got it."

When she walks away Eric says, "So—you look extra cheerful this morning. What's up?"

"Nothing," I say as I take a drink of the coffee the waitress just set down in front of me. "I've just had a good couple of days."

"With Gabby?" Eric asks with a grin.

"Yes, with Gabby," I say.

"I'm glad you're finally getting back out there," Eric says. "It's nice to see you happy again."

"Well, we're not rushing anything, but we are dating."

"I'm happy for you."

Our food arrives and we dig into our breakfasts of eggs and bacon with toast. "It seems like you've been spending a lot of time with Alyssa," I tease. "Looked like you two were enjoying yourselves at the festival the other night."

"Yeah, well—strictly friends," Eric says as he takes another bite. "I gave up on being anything more a long time ago. She can't handle anything more than friendship with someone in my profession—and I love my job."

"Still, I've never known *you* to give up."

"Usually I wouldn't. But I value my friendship with Alyssa too much to do anything that would screw it up."

"Come on—you and Alyssa are great friends. I highly doubt you would screw it up by pursuing her," I say.

"I wouldn't be too sure about that. I think it's hard enough for her to be friends with me when she knows I go to work every day and there's a chance I may not come home. For her to be in a relationship with me, that worry would be even worse. I'm just afraid if I ask her out, she'll think I'm heartless for even suggesting it since I know what happened to her brother."

I shake my head. "I don't think she would ever think you're heartless. You're the one that convinced me to open up again and give things a shot with Gabby. So I'm not going to let you sit back and hide behind your fear either. You need to just ask Alyssa out."

"I'll think about it."

"Alright, fair enough. So—you have any plans for the rest of the day?"

"Nah. Probably just go home to take a nap and relax in front of the TV. What about you?"

"Gabby and I have plans this afternoon."

"Do you now?" Eric teases with a chuckle.

"We're going to hang out by the water. Maybe go on a sightseeing cruise."

"That'll be fun and it's a beautiful day for a cruise." Eric and I finish our breakfast and pay for our meals before making our way out of the diner. "Enjoy your date!" Eric says as he climbs into his car.

"Thanks. Enjoy your nap. Talk to you later." As I walk to my truck, I pull my cell phone out of my pocket and call Gabby.

"Hello?" she answers.

"Hey, Gabby. I just finished breakfast with Eric. What time do you want to head down to the lakeshore? I think there's a sightseeing tour at two o'clock."

"Okay. That would be great! I'm thinking we could head down to the water at noon, then? That should give us plenty of time to walk around and make it to the dock, right?" Gabby asks.

"Yeah, that should be good. I'll pick you up around eleven forty-five."

"Sounds great! I'll see you then!" she says happily.

"See you then," I say.

Hanging up my phone, I climb into my truck and

turn the key. The engine sputters loudly before dying out. "Aww, shit!" I curse as I slam my hand against the steering wheel. I grab the jump starter from behind my seat and climb back out of the truck. I attach the cables to the battery and turn the jump starter on. When I try to start the ignition again, nothing happens.

After calling a tow truck, I call Gabby back while I wait for it to arrive. "Hey, Gabby. So—slight problem. My truck won't start. I've tried jumping it and called for a tow, but it looks like I won't be able to pick you up after all."

"I'm sorry about your truck, but no worries. I'll come pick you up instead," she says.

"You don't mind?" I ask.

"Of course not! Where should I pick you up?"

"Could you pick me up at Murphy's Cafe? I'll just have the tow truck bring my truck to the garage for me and check in with them later. I can wait here."

"Sure, no problem!" she says. "I'll pick you up soon."

"Okay, thanks Gabby." Hanging up the phone, there's nothing to do now except wait.

*W*hen I arrive at Murphy's Cafe a short while later, I see the tow truck hooking Brandon's truck up to the back. Pulling into a parking spot a few spaces over, I wave.

"Hey," he says in surprise. "I wasn't expecting you to be here until eleven forty-five."

"Yeah, well, I figured I wouldn't make you wait. I assumed the tow wouldn't take long to get here," I say.

"Thanks," Brandon says with a smile.

"You're welcome." Once his truck has been towed away, he walks over to my SUV and jumps in. "So how has your day been so far—besides having issues with the truck, I mean."

"It's been good. I was able to catch up with Eric over breakfast a little," Brandon says.

"That's good. Oh—I forgot to ask you. Do we need to make reservations for the sightseeing cruise or are we able to just show up?"

"To be honest, I haven't been on one of the cruises in years. I'm not really sure. We should probably make a reservation just to be on the safe side."

"Alright." I pull my cell phone out and pull up the website for the cruises. Finding the one at two o'clock, I select it and choose the option to make a reservation. After entering all of our information I say, "There. That was easy enough."

I pull out of the parking lot and we drive down to the lakeshore, parking in the lot for sightseeing cruises. We're still early so there aren't many cars here yet. Climbing out, Brandon meets me on my side and takes my hand as we make our way down towards the water. The tiny waves are gently lapping against the shore as we kick off our shoes and walk along the beach. The upper half of the beach is sandy, but turns into rocks the closer you get to the water— so we stay in the sandy part. Small patches of snow still dot the shoreline, not yet melted, and the water that manages to reach our feet is absolutely frigid, but the warm sun shining down makes for a beautiful late spring day.

"Is Lake Superior always this beautiful?" I ask as I look out over the clear, sparkling water.

Brandon shakes his head. "It can get pretty rough and the waves can be insanely high. Especially around November. The water turns really dark and frothy, you can actually hear the waves violently crashing against anything that gets in their way."

"I think I remember hearing something about that," I say as I recall hearing about shipwrecks that have happened on the lake.

We continue to walk down the beach a little ways before Brandon kneels down and looks at where the sand meets the rocks. "What's wrong?" I ask.

"Nothing's wrong," he says smiling up at me. "I just happened to spot this." He holds a small rock out to me in the palm of his hand.

"You spotted a rock?" I ask with a confused expression. "There are tons of rocks."

Brandon laughs. "Not just any rock—it's an agate."

"Oh!" I say as I take the rock to inspect it closer. It has a pink color with white bands swirled around it. "Wow—that's really cool. I don't think I've ever actually seen an agate in person—only in books."

"There are quite a few of them here. If you ever look out your window and see a ton of people on the beach walking and looking at the ground, they are probably agate hunting."

"Actually I *have* seen that a few times. I wondered

what they were all doing."

Chuckling, Brandon says, "Yeah—a lot of people up here like to collect them. Some even make jewelry out of them."

"Understandable. I can see how they would make really pretty jewelry."

As I'm about to hand the agate back to Brandon he says, "No, you keep it. That way you'll have one to look at in person whenever you want."

"Thanks," I say with a smile.

Brandon's phone starts to chime and he pulls it out of his pocket. "That's the alarm I set for he cruise. We should probably turn around and head back towards the dock so we don't miss it."

"Sounds good."

Turning around, we walk back the way we came and make it to the dock for the sightseeing cruise just in time for boarding to begin. I find the confirmation email on my phone and show it to the man at the entrance. "Perfect. You two are all set. Enjoy your cruise!" he says as he hands my phone back to me.

We step onto a yacht style boat with three levels. The bottom two levels are both indoors while the top level is open air. Glancing through the windows of the lower deck, there is a bar and a seating area, as well as a snack bar. A few people are gathered around getting refreshments.

Brandon and I walk along the deck and climb the stairs to the third level of the ship, to the top viewing deck. It's set up with tables and padded chairs for guests to sit at, and has a small concession stand in the back. We find a table along the side where we think we'll have the best view and sit down.

A few of the seats around us fill up as other guests arrive for the cruise, but since it's the off-season it's not too crowded. As I glance around, I see my realtor Samantha waving to me as she makes her way towards our table. "Gabby! It's great to see you again. I see you finally decided to take a sightseeing cruise!" she says.

"Hi, Samantha. Yeah, it's such a beautiful day today that we thought a cruise would be fun."

Samantha does a double take as she realizes who is sitting beside me. "Oh! I'm so sorry Brandon. I—I didn't recognize you at first. How are you?" she asks.

"I'm good thanks," Brandon says with a smile as he puts his arm around my shoulders.

"I'm glad to hear it," Samantha says. "How are you liking Wilkins Harbor, Gabby?"

"I love it! It's been a huge change from what I was used to, that's for sure, but I'm so glad I moved here," I say.

"Good. Well—I better head to my table. We should be pushing off soon. Good seeing you both!"

she says as she waves and walks to the table where the rest of her group is sitting. A few minutes later the captain makes an announcement that we are all set to depart.

The ship slowly backs away from the dock and begins making its way further out from the shore. We cruise along while the captain points out different locations. There are popular swimming beaches where we see families happily playing in the water, as well as the shiny dome on top of the monastery. We pass by the Seafood Palace and several local tourist shops on our way towards the lighthouse. The waves gently rock the ship as we sail past beautiful Victorian style homes surrounded by flowers.

"Wow—these homes are beautiful," I say in awe as I admire them.

"Yeah, they really are. Wait until you see them at Christmastime," Brandon says. "The owner's deck them out with lights and decorations, both inside and out. They're always part of the Tour of Homes."

"What's that?" I ask curiously.

"It's a tour that happens once a year. Homes that participate go all out for decorations. They open their homes to the public on one specific night for everyone to tour the insides. There's usually refreshments at each and they tell you about the history of the homes."

"That sounds amazing!"

"Yeah, it is a lot of fun. I remember going with my parents and grandparents when I was younger."

As we round a bend past the lighthouse, Edwards Mansion comes into view. The flower gardens are full of beautifully blooming flowers in every color imaginable. Even from here, I can see the bubbling water fountain in the center of the garden. We can see guests sitting in the sunroom enjoying this gorgeous afternoon. "Edwards Mansion looks so grand from here," I say.

"You're right, it does."

"I'm so glad we decided to come on this cruise. I'm seeing Wilkins Harbor in a completely different way." We continue to pass by the breathtaking homes along the shoreline before coming to a place that has a white gazebo with a golden dome. The rails are wrapped with garlands of brightly colored daisies— hot pink, red, yellow, orange, and purple. White tulle is draped between the beams in an elegant way and in the center stands a happy bride and groom celebrating their wedding day. "So beautiful."

"That's a very popular location for summer weddings here. The couple that owns the property rents the gazebo out every year and they even allow the bridal party to stay in their guest home for a few nights if they want to."

"Wow. That's very generous of them."

"Yeah, it is. But they absolutely love doing it," Brandon says with a smile. As the ship makes a turn to begin the trip back to the dock, he asks, "Would you like anything from the concession stand? I was thinking that an ice cream sounds good right about now."

"Sure! I never turn down ice cream! I love it!" I say excitedly.

"Any particular flavor?"

"Nope! I treat all ice cream equally. Surprise me."

Brandon chuckles. "Alright. I'll be right back." He kisses the top of my head as he makes his way to the back of the ship to get us some. When he returns a few minutes later he's carrying a large bowl with two spoons. "I hope you don't mind—I figured we could share."

"I don't mind sharing. What flavor did you get?"

"Mackinac Island Fudge."

"Yum! I've never been to the island, but Alyssa brought me fudge from there one time when we were in college."

"Oh, yeah? I forgot you two were roommates." Brandon takes a bite of the sweet treat and says, "You should add Mackinac Island to your bucket list of places to go. It's really beautiful and there are a lot of cool things to see and do on the island."

"Okay, but only if you come with me." I smile at him and bat my eyelashes.

"Deal!" Brandon says with a chuckle.

The ship pulls up to the dock and the captain makes an announcement over the speaker. "This is your Captain. On behalf of all of us with Keweenaw Tours, I want to thank you for touring with us today. We hope you had a wonderful cruise."

Brandon and I make our way off of the ship and back onto shore. "So what did you think of the tour?" Brandon asks.

"The tour was great! I'm really glad we decided to do this today."

"I'm glad we did too. Let's stop in here really quick," Brandon says as he guides me into a small shop near the dock.

"Okay." I follow him into the shop and look around. As I browse through the racks of souvenirs, Brandon disappears. He returns a moment later holding a small gift bag.

"What's this?" I ask as he hands it to me.

"Open it."

He smiles as I open the bag and pull out a beautiful agate necklace. "Oh, wow! Brandon, it's beautiful! Thank you!"

"You're welcome. Here—let me help you put it on."

He hooks the necklace around my neck before I turn and give him a quick kiss. When we're finished in the shop I ask, "Should I drive you home, or do I need to bring you to the repair shop for your truck?"

"I should probably go to the shop to see if my truck is ready. If you don't mind driving me there, that is."

"Nope, not at all."

We walk to my SUV and climb in before making the drive to the repair shop. When we arrive, I pull up to the front of the garage and park. Brandon says, "Mind waiting if I run inside really quick to see if it's ready?"

"Sure, I can wait."

Brandon walks inside and returns a few minutes later, coming up to my side of the vehicle. I roll down my window to see what's going on. "My truck is all set, so I can drive home from here. I'll see you tomorrow?"

"Yep!" I say with a smile.

"Okay," Brandon says as he leans in my window and gives me a kiss. "Drive home safe."

"I will." After giving him one more kiss, I back out of my parking spot and wave as he climbs into his own truck. As I drive home, I happily sing along with the radio. Today was an amazing day seeing all of the sights, and Brandon makes me incredibly happy.

Chapter Sixteen

BRANDON

*T*hree weeks later....

Gabby and I have been dating for a couple of weeks now and even though it's been only a short amount of time, my heart finally feels whole again. A part of me will always miss Olivia, but Gabby makes me happy, and I know that Olivia would want me to find love again. I haven't enjoyed myself or felt this good in a really long time and this is nice.

When Gabby's finished with her shift, she comes with me to my apartment. I lock the door behind us, "Why don't you go pick out a movie and I'll grab us some snacks?"

"Okay," she says.

I head into the kitchen as Gabby walks over and kneels down in front of the shelves of movies I have in the corner. Opening the pantry door, I pull out a bag of popcorn and place it in the microwave before grabbing two bottles of water out of the refrigerator. When the timer goes off on the microwave, I pull the bag out and empty its contents into a large bowl. Carrying the snacks into the living room, I set them on the coffee table and sit down on the couch to wait for Gabby. "Are you seeing anything that looks good?" I ask.

"I think so!" Gabby says as she stands up with her selection and joins me on the couch. "Have you watched *Skyfall* lately?"

"Not recently, but I like that one. That's a great James Bond film. Though—Really? You're into that kind of movie?" I ask, raising my eyebrows.

"Yeah, I love action movies. My preferred genre is usually horror or romance—depending on what kind of mood I'm in—but action movies are good too."

"Works for me then." Standing up, I take the movie from Gabby and put it into the blu-ray player. When I sit back down next to her on the couch, I grab the bowl of popcorn and put it between us. We settle in and start the movie.

Halfway through, when we're done with the popcorn, I set the bowl back on the table and lean back. As the movie plays on in the background I can't help but pull Gabby in closer. The sweet raspberry scent of her hair tickles my nose as I lean in and plant a kiss on her neck. I feel her shiver at my touch, as a hum escapes her throat. "Brandon—that's very distracting," she says as she smiles at me.

"Mmm—I bet it is," I say as I continue to pepper kisses along her neck and behind her ear. I twist my fingers into her hair, tugging her head gently back so that I can kiss her lips. As I slide my tongue into her mouth, one of her hands reaches up and wraps around the back of my neck while the other grips the front of my shirt. "I think we should move upstairs to the bedroom," I murmur against her lips.

"Are you sure?" she asks. "I mean—are you sure you want this?"

"Oh, trust me. I'm sure," I say with a chuckle. "Come here," I say as I gently scoop her up onto my lap and wrap her legs around my waist.

Standing, I carry her up the stairs and to the bedroom. I lay Gabby down on the bed and kiss her once more before stepping back to admire the sight of her in my bed. I grip the hem of my shirt and pull it up over my head before kneeling on the bed with one leg on each side of her. Gabby reaches up and runs her fingers down my chest, trailing them down along my abs. I tremble at the feel of her skin against mine. My breathing quickens as her fingers travel lower, playing with the button on my jeans. I suck in a breath as her fingertip dips below the waistline of my pants.

I pull Gabby's shirt up and over her head as I lean forward, kissing her lips with mine. Slowly, I kiss down her neck and to her breast. I slide the lacy fabric of her bra to the side and take her breast into my mouth. "Oh!" she gasps.

Reaching behind her back, I unclasp her bra with one hand and tug it off, tossing it onto the floor. As she lay beneath me, bare chested, I can feel her shaking with anticipation. Smiling, I skim my tongue over her skin, nipping gently. She squirms as she pants, "Brandon! That's driving me crazy!"

Chuckling, I grin up at her and say, "If *that's* driving you crazy, you better brace yourself because I'm just getting started." I unbutton her jeans and slide them off, leaving her in just her lacy panties. I kiss her through the fabric before gently tugging them off and exploring her with my tongue. "Oh, Gabby—you're already dripping wet for me," I say as she moans and tugs at my hair.

"Brandon, I want you," Gabby says. "Please." She reaches for the button of my jeans and fumbles with it for a minute before I help her out and push my pants down.

"How badly do you want me, Gabby?" I tease.

"Please Brandon. I want to feel you inside of me," she pleads.

Slowly, I push into her—a little at a time—letting her adjust to the intrusion. "You feel nice! You're so tight," I gasp as she clenches around me. She rocks her hips into mine, causing me to push deeper. I bite my lip and groan at the sensation that comes from being buried so deep inside of her.

"You like that?" Gabby asks as she rocks her hips up into mine again and again.

"Uhh—" I nod yes as the pleasure I feel has caused me to lose the ability to form coherent words. I was the one that told Gabby to brace herself, but apparently it's me that should be bracing. Tangling my legs around hers, I flip us so that she's on top. She grinds her hips against me as her silky hair fans around her face. "Gabby. You're going to make me explode if you keep doing that."

"Mmmm—what about if I do *this*?" she asks as she slides up until we're almost completely separated before thrusting herself back down.

"Oh shit!" I pant as I grip her hips and hold her down. "Definitely going to make me explode that way."

She smiles as she bends down to kiss me, gripping my hands above my head as we rock together. As our tongues taste each other in a passionate kiss, our bodies move in the perfect rhythm. She releases my hands and I slide my fingers between us to explore her as we continue grinding and thrusting. "Oh!" she moans at the added stimulation. "Brandon!"

"I love hearing you say my name," I say as I thrust into her a few more times, sending us both over the edge.

Gabby collapses on top of me and I fold my arms around her. I kiss the top of her head as we lay on my bed, sweaty and tired. She traces her fingers lazily in a pattern on my chest and I can feel her smiling. "This was not what I was expecting when you invited me over for a movie night," she says.

Chuckling I say, "It's not exactly what I had planned either, but—I've got no complaints."

"Me neither," Gabby says happily.

After resting together for a while, Gabby goes to use the bathroom while I dispose of the condom and throw on my boxers. When she returns, I pull her back down onto the bed next to me. "So—do you absolutely need to go home tonight? Or would you like to stay here?"

"Do you want me to stay here?" she asks, searching my face for an answer.

"Yeah—I *do*," I say as I tilt her chin up to give her a kiss.

She thinks for a minute before hesitantly answering, "Alright. As long as you're sure. I don't want you to feel pressured into letting me spend the night or feel like we're moving too fast or—"

"Gabby," I say, silencing her with a kiss. "*I'm* the one who asked you to stay. I promise—I want you to."

"Okay." She smiles at me before settling herself in against my side, laying her head against my chest. Wrapping one arm around her I pull the blankets up around both of us with the other and rest my chin on top of her head. I feel my body relaxing as I listen to the quiet sound of her breathing and feel her warmth against me. For the first time in a long time, I fall into a deep sleep holding a beautiful woman in my arms.

I can hear birds chirping and feel the warmth of the sun streaming in through the window against my still closed eyelids as I wake up feeling well rested. I don't think I've slept that well in ages. Opening my eyes, I blink a few times to adjust to the light. Brandon is still asleep next to me with his arm draped across my stomach.

Smiling to myself, I take a minute to admire his sleeping form. His black hair is slightly mussed, his mouth is slightly open, and he looks so peaceful. I need to go to the bathroom, but he's sleeping so soundly that I don't want to wake him. I gently try to slide out from under his arm. Brandon's grip around my waist tightens and he pulls me into his side, murmuring, "Where are you going?"

"Bathroom. I'll be right back—go back to sleep,"

I say quietly. Sliding out of bed I head to the bath-room. When I'm finished, I tiptoe back into the bedroom and crawl back into bed beside him.

"Feel better now?" he asks sleepily as he wraps his arms around me again.

"Much." I snuggle into his hold and rest my head against his chest.

Brandon kisses the top of my head and whispers, "I like waking up with you in my arms."

Looking up at him, I place my hand on his face and say, "I like waking up in them." I gently pull his face down to meet mine and kiss him softly. His tongue slips into my mouth as he deepens the kiss, fully awake now. He runs his hand up and down my side and I shudder with his touch. Pulling apart, I moan as Brandon kisses his way from my mouth, down my jaw, my neck, and to my chest. He looks up at me with his beautiful green eyes as he flicks his tongue out across my breast. His hand caresses my other breast, and I can feel the smile on his lips as I begin to writhe beneath him.

"Mmm—I like making you squirm," he says. Sliding down, he plants kisses along my inner thigh. "Should I keep going?" he asks.

"Yes! Please," I beg.

As soon as his tongue hits me, my hands fly into his hair as waves of sensation wash over me. Brandon swirls his tongue around as he slowly pushes a finger inside my entrance. "You're *so* wet for me," he says in between licks.

"I want you, Brandon," I say breathlessly as he keeps edging me closer and closer to an intense orgasm. "Come here." I tug at him as he wipes his mouth and slides up to kiss me. As he does, I reach down to grab him, and stroke him. His breathing speeds up and he moans into my mouth.

"Oh fuck, Gabby!"

"Lie down," I say as I push him onto his back. As I continue to stroke him, I move down so that I can tease him with my tongue. I lick and suck him into my mouth.

"Fuck, baby," Brandon hisses as I can feel him trembling. He tangles his fingers in my hair as I move my head up and down, and continue stroking him with my hand. "Baby, I want to be inside of you."

I suck him into my mouth once more, before reaching for a condom on his side table and opening it. After rolling it on, I line him up with my entrance before sliding down onto him. Rocking my hips up and down slowly, I take him inch by inch. He slides in a little more with each movement until he is fully buried inside.

Brandon grabs my hips as he thrusts into me. I can feel my walls tightening around him as I beg for more. We're both breathing hard as we rock and thrust together in a synchronized rhythm. Tangling his legs with mine, Brandon rolls us so he's on top and continues to pump into me—harder and faster with each movement. I wrap my legs around him and claw at his back as an orgasm rips through me. With a few more thrusts he calls out my name with his own release.

Brandon gently collapses on top of me, supporting most of his weight with his forearms, before rolling off and lying next to me. Brushing a piece of sweaty hair out of my face and smiling, he says, "Good morning, beautiful. That was a nice way to wake up."

"Definitely the best way to wake up," I giggle.

He kisses my forehead and hugs me close for a few minutes. "You know—now that I'm awake, I should probably take a shower," he says as he wiggles his eyebrows.

"Yeah, you probably should. You kinda stink," I tease.

"Hey, that's not very nice," he says as he tickles me until I'm giggling and squirming.

"Alright, alright," I say between giggles. "You win —let's both shower."

He climbs off of the bed and helps me up so we can head into the bathroom to shower. We end up making love several more times throughout the day before finally admitting that we're both exhausted. Our relationship started out slow and now it seems like we just can't get enough of each other.

Later while we're snuggled in bed watching TV on the small screen set up on his dresser, Brandon says, "I don't remember the last time I spent all day in bed."

"Well technically we didn't spend *all* day in bed," I say with a smirk. "There was also the shower, the kitchen counter, and a few other places."

He chuckles and nods. "You're right—I guess that counts as getting out of bed. But what I meant was that I don't remember the last time I didn't go over to the inn, or run errands, or do something else to keep myself busy."

I rub my hand against his chest where my head is resting. "Everyone deserves a break sometimes. Even you."

"Yeah. I guess it was just easier for me to keep myself busy all the time so I didn't think about the accident. But you've helped me to heal, Gabby. You've helped me to feel whole again."

I smile up at Brandon and give him a kiss. It warms my heart to hear him say that I've made him feel whole. When I first met him, I didn't think that he would ever be able to open up to me, or anyone for that matter. And I didn't know if I'd ever be able to trust a man again, but Brandon has shown me that it's possible. "You've helped me too," I say quietly.

"What do you mean?" he asks.

Besides a handful of people, I haven't told anyone what happened in Arizona with Tim. Taking a deep breath I say, "I don't want to get into all of the details right now and ruin this perfect night, but let's just say that I had some issues with my ex. I didn't think I would ever be able to trust men again, but you've shown me that I can."

"Well, then I'm glad that I was able to help you too. You can always trust me, Gabby. I'll never do anything to hurt you or break that trust." He gives me a gentle squeeze and I sigh contentedly. For the rest of the night we lie in bed, holding each other, and enjoying just being together. And for the second night in a row I fall asleep in his arms.

The last two days have been amazing. Gabby and I have spent almost every minute together, and I have never felt so happy. I woke up this morning with her in my arms again and we had a nice breakfast together before she left to go home to change clothes before work. She's working the afternoon shift at Edwards Mansion, and I have the day off so that I can go fishing with my grandfather, but we've made plans to spend the night at her place tonight.

After loading all of my fishing gear into my truck, I drive around to the inn and park in the lot. Even though I have the day off, I want to stop in quick to make sure that nothing needs my attention. I walk through the doors and to the front desk to talk to Chloe. "Good morning, Chloe."

"Good morning, Mr. Edwards," Chloe says with a smile.

I cringe at the use of my full name. As many times as I've told her to call me Brandon, Chloe is still my only employee that calls me Mr. Edwards. Pushing my annoyance aside I say, "I'm about to head out for the day to go fishing, but I wanted to make sure that everything here is good first. Is there anything that you need? Any issues that I need to know about?"

"No, everything is good here! I can't think of anything. So—have a good day off!"

"Thanks, Chloe." I turn to walk out of the lobby. On my way out, I hold the door open for an elderly couple who are our newest arrivals. I greet them and welcome them to the inn before walking out to my truck and heading to my grandparents' house.

As I drive, I sing along to a country song on the radio and enjoy the fresh air blowing in through my open window. The temperature is getting warmer each day, and today is particularly hot. When I arrive at my grandparents' house I see my grandmother out front working in her flower garden. "Hi, Grandma!" I say as I step out of my truck.

"Oh, hi Brandon!" she says as she pauses what she's doing and turns around to greet me. "Are you all set to go fishing with your grandfather? He's been eagerly waiting to go all morning. Not very patiently I might add."

I chuckle, knowing that he's probably been driving her nuts muttering about how the fish won't be biting if we don't go soon. "Yeah, I'm ready. Sorry I'm so late. I slept in a little and then had to check on a few things at the inn before I came over."

Grandma gets a knowing gleam in her eye as she asks, "Slept in, huh? Since when do *you* sleep in?"

"Alright, alright," I say holding my hands up in surrender. "I was having breakfast with Gabby." No use hiding it from her—Grandma would probably hear it from someone else around town, if she hasn't already, that I'm dating Gabby now. It's a small town after all, and everyone knows each others' business.

"Um-hum. I thought it might be the case that you were with Gabby. I heard from some of the ladies at my weekly bridge game that they've seen you around town with a pretty little brunette."

"Of course you did," I say with a laugh as I shake my head.

"I'm so happy for you Brandon. Gabby seems like a sweet girl, and you deserve to be happy again."

"Thanks, Grandma." I give her a hug. "I better let Grandpa know I'm here."

"Yeah, you better. Otherwise he's going to go without you. That man is so impatient sometimes," she says teasingly. "He's probably out back by the dock."

"Alright. I'll see you later, Grandma." I grab my fishing gear out of my truck and head around to the back of the house. Sure enough, Grandpa is on the dock getting the boat ready. "Hey, Grandpa! Need any help?" I ask as I join him on the dock.

"About time you got here. We'll be lucky if any of the fish are still biting—morning fishing is always better than whatever time it is now!" he says half jokingly.

"Sorry Grandpa."

"Ahh," he says waving his hand, "it's alright. I'm just giving you a hard time. We'll still have a nice day out on the water."

I help my grandpa finish getting the boat ready and load our gear. We both climb in and push off, waving to my grandma who took a break from gardening and came out back to see us off. Grandpa drives the boat out to a small cove that has become our fishing spot since shortly after he and grandma retired. He turns off the outboard motor and we grab our fishing poles. As I grab a worm from the container and bait my hook I ask my grandpa, "So— are we making our usual wager? Whoever catches the most fish wins? Loser buys a round of drinks next time you join Eric and I at the bar?"

"Sounds good to me. Are you sure *you* want to, seeing as you've ended up buying drinks the last couple of times?" Grandpa teases.

"I'm feeling lucky today," I say with a grin as I cast my line.

"Oh, yeah?" asks Grandpa as he casts his. "And why is that?"

"No reason."

"You sure about that? Sure it doesn't have anything to do with a certain young woman?"

"Maybe." I can't help but smile as I think about Gabby.

"That's what I thought."

We fall into a comfortable silence as we spend the next couple of hours fishing. The water is calm, and the sun shining down on us feels fantastic. There's relatively little wind today, so it's a wonderful day to be out. Once the fish stop biting in our little cove we decide to troll our way back to the house. We each catch a few more fish along the way. When we arrive at the dock, I lean over to tie the boat up as my grandpa steers it in.

Grandma is sitting on the back deck and waves as we step out of the boat with our fishing poles. As we walk up to the house she asks, "How was fishing?"

"Great as always," Grandpa says. "Although, it

looks like I'll be buying a round of drinks sometime soon."

Grandma smiles. "Caught more fish than Grandpa today, Brandon?"

"Yes, ma'am," I say with a chuckle. "I warned him that I was feeling lucky today, but he still took the bet."

"Of course I did! I would never back down on the chance to beat you at fishing," Grandpa says as he pats my shoulder. "We've been doing that contest since you were old enough to drink."

"True. More often now that you're retired."

"Damn right!" Grandpa says with a laugh.

"I'm guessing I should fire up the grill for a fish dinner tonight?" Grandma asks.

"You know it," Grandpa says. He pulls the fish out of the live well, and carries them over to our cleaning station. Once they have been properly cleaned, he brings our fish inside to wrap mine up for me and put his in the refrigerator until dinner.

"What about you, Brandon? Will you stay and join us for dinner?" she asks as she stands up to start the grill.

"I'd love to, but I already have plans with Gabby. Can I take a raincheck?"

"Of course you can, dear. Next time be sure to

bring her with you. She can keep me company while you and Grandpa go fishing."

"I think she'd like that," I say. "Enjoy your dinner and I'll see you both again soon, alright?"

"Don't forget to take your fish," Grandpa says as he comes back outside and gives me a hug goodbye.

"I won't. Thanks." I grab the cooler with my fish and give Grandma a hug. After walking to my truck I open the door, and place the cooler in the passenger side before climbing into the driver's seat. I send a quick text to Gabby asking her if she wants fresh fish fry for dinner before I start the drive home.

Stopping by my place first to take a quick shower, I place the fish in the freezer, leaving just enough for tonight in the cooler. I run upstairs and shower before packing an overnight bag to take to Gabby's. As I make my way back downstairs, I glance at my phone and see that Gabby texted me back.

Gabby: Yes! Fresh fish fry sounds fantastic!

I type out a response as I grab the cooler off of the counter.

Me: Perfect! Heading over now. See you in a few minutes.

Tossing my bag and the cooler into the truck, I hop in and drive to her house. When I pull into the driveway, she opens the front door and waits for me on the veranda.

"Hey!" she greets me with a smile. "How was fishing? You must have caught some for us to eat."

"It was great! Grandpa was a little miffed that I was late getting there, but he got over it once he saw that the fish were still biting. We had a nice couple of hours out on the water. Plus—I beat him at catching the most fish."

Gabby laughs. "You sound pretty proud about beating your grandpa."

Chuckling, I say, "I am. He's won the bet the last couple of times. It's about time he pay up."

"Bet, huh? And what exactly does the loser have to do?" she asks as she leads me inside.

"Buy a round of drinks at the bar."

"Ah, I see," she says.

"My grandma said you need to come with next time. She said you can hang out with her while my grandpa and I fish." I set the cooler down on the floor in her kitchen.

"I'd love to!"

"Good. Now, enough about my grandparents," I say as I pull her in for a kiss. She wraps her arms around my neck as I wrap mine around her waist, backing her up against the counter. She squeaks as I lift her onto the counter.

"What are you doing?" Gabby giggles.

"Mmm—I'm kissing you," I say as I kiss down her neck. "I missed you today."

"I missed you too." She gently cups my chin in her hand and pulls my face up so our eyes meet. "But I'm *starving*, so let's eat first. We can have some fun later tonight."

Chuckling, I say, "Alright. You win. Let's eat first." I grip her waist and help her slide down onto the floor. She gives me one more kiss before we work together to make a delicious meal.

*A*fter dinner, Brandon and I move into the living room and sit down on the couch. "That fresh trout was amazing! You pan fried it perfectly. Thanks for sharing with me," I say as he hands me a glass of Chardonnay.

"Of course. I'm glad you enjoyed it."

"So—now that I'm no longer starving, I wouldn't be opposed to what you started in the kitchen," I say with a grin.

Brandon laughs. "You wouldn't be opposed?" He leans in to kiss me before he whispers in my ear, "So you wouldn't have any complaints if I did *this*?" His hand slowly slides under my shirt to cup my breast.

"No, no complaints," I say as my body tingles from his touch.

He kisses down my neck and my head falls back, while I enjoy the sensations his kisses are creating. "What about this?" he asks as he trails his hand lower, dipping below the waistline of my panties.

"Mmmm, nope."

His fingers graze against my most sensitive area before he slips a finger inside, collecting my wetness, and then circling me again. "You want more?" he asks.

"Yes," I say breathlessly as my body begins to quiver.

"Mmmm, come here then," he says as he picks me up and carries me to the bedroom. He gently sets me down on the bed before stepping back and pulling his shirt over his head and tugging off his jeans and boxers. Crawling on top of me he says, "Now where was I? Oh yes—"

He slides my jeans and panties down my legs and pulls them off before lowering his head and pleasuring me with his tongue. I nearly jump off the bed with the intense sensation. He alternates between sucks and flicks of his tongue as he drives me higher. With a few more licks, I'm careening over the edge.

As I lay panting for breath he slowly sits up and wipes his mouth with the back of his hand. "Still no complaints?" he asks with a smile.

"Definitely no complaints."

"Good." Taking himself in his hand and stroking a few times, he lines himself up with my entrance. He thrusts into me with one quick, fluid movement. "Damn, you feel good," he growls.

I rake my fingernails down his back as he thrusts into me, again and again. I roll my hips to match his rhythm, changing the angle just a bit. He sucks in a ragged breath as his movements become more irregular.

"Oh, fuck, Gabby. That's going to push me over the edge."

"Good thing I like pushing you over the edge then," I say, grinding my hips up into him again. With a couple more thrusts, Brandon and I are both crying out in pleasure.

Brandon gently rolls off and cuddles next to me, holding me in his arms as we both recover from our lovemaking. After a few minutes, he says, "I could really get used to this you know."

"Used to what?"

"Waking up with you in my arms every morning and falling asleep with you in my arms every night. Plus everything in between."

I smile up at him. "I could get used to it, too." And that's the truth—I really could get used to this.

Waking up with Brandon every morning and being with him every night. I feel like nothing in the world can come between us. We spend the night relaxing together and finally fall asleep in each other's arms, not knowing what tomorrow will bring, but hoping that it will be another day filled with happiness.

Chapter Twenty

BRANDON

After waking up at Gabby's this morning, we got ready and came into work together. She has a shift baking this morning, and I want to get some work done in my office. After a few hours of sifting through financials and other documents on my computer, I reach into my filing cabinet and pull out some papers. As I sit at my desk finishing the necessary paperwork, my phone chimes with a text message.

Eric: Hey! When do you and Gabby get off of work today?
Me: In about ten minutes. Why?
Eric: It's such a nice day today. Alyssa and I are going to the beach. Do you and Gabby want to come?

Me: I'll ask her. Why don't you and Alyssa meet us in the garden in about fifteen minutes and we'll let you know then?
Eric: Sounds good! See you soon!

Putting the paperwork into the filing cabinet under my desk, I stand up and stretch before walking out to kitchen. On my way there, I spot Gabby placing baked goods in the coffee corner, and happily chatting with some guests who have been staying at the inn the last couple of days.

"Have a wonderful lunch!" she says as they say their goodbyes and walk out the door. She sees me walking towards her and smiles. "Hey, you. I thought you were drowning in paperwork in the office," she teases.

"Ha ha, very funny," I say with a chuckle. "Eric just texted me. He and Alyssa are going to the beach and want to know if you and I want to join them."

"Sure! What time do they want to go?"

"They're meeting us here in about fifteen—well ten, now—minutes," I say as I glance at my watch.

"Oh! Okay. Well—I just need to run home quick to change into my swimsuit, but as long as they don't mind stopping there first or meeting us at the beach, I'm in!"

"Great. I'm going to run to my place to change and then I'll be right back, okay?"

"Sounds good."

I hurry to my house and change into my swim trunks, grab a towel, toss a few drinks into a cooler, and head back to the inn to pick up Gabby. She's just gathering her things and saying goodbye to Chloe when I arrive. "You ready to go?" I ask.

"Yep! All set."

I take her hand in mine and lead her outside. We're walking through the flower garden in front of the inn when Gabby suddenly freezes in place. She squeezes my hand, gripping so tightly that it's almost painful. "Gabby? Are you alright?"

She shakes her head no and I can feel her shaking beside me. I follow her gaze across the lawn and see a man stalking angrily towards us. I stiffen and step slightly in front of her as I wonder who this man is.

As he moves closer I hear him shout, "Hey! Think you could hide from me, bitch?!"

Gabby whimpers beside me. "Gabby? Who is that?"

The man continues to yell and curse. Out of the corner of my eye I see guests who were out for a stroll quickly walk in the opposite direction—clearly sensing danger. "I told you what would happen if you opened your mouth, Gabby! No one else needs to be involved," he says, nodding in my direction.

"Brandon—I think you should go back inside,"

she says shakily with tears streaming down her face.
She tries to step around me, but I hold her firmly
behind.

"I'm not leaving you, Gabby. But what the hell is
going on?" I ask, keeping my eyes on the approaching
man.

Gabby quietly whispers, "That's my ex—Tim. I
came to Wilkins Harbor to—"

"Shut up, Gabby!" the man, Tim, shouts. "I'm sick
of you not listening to me! I warned you! I went to
jail once already because of you, little bitch! That's
not going to happen again."

My heart thunders in my chest as I see him pull a
gun out from behind his back. My mind races as I try
to process what's happening. I wasn't able to protect
Olivia and prevent her death, but I'm damn sure
going to do everything I can to protect Gabby. I have
my concealed carry weapon on me, but quickly glancing, I can see that there are too many people around
to safely shoot it. I don't want any innocent
bystanders to get hurt.

Everything seems to move in slow motion as the
gun goes off and I push Gabby out of the way. Sharp
pain courses through my shoulder as the bullet hits
me. I can feel my shirt getting wet as sticky, warm
blood oozes out. I see Eric, who I didn't notice

before, pull out his gun, and hear him yell for Tim to put his weapon down.

Sirens seem to grow closer as I slowly fall to the ground, and I realize that someone must have called the police. Gabby screams and cries as she drops to her knees beside me, holding her hands over the wound in my shoulder. I'm vaguely aware of a commotion going on around me as police arrest Tim —who's already disarmed and in cuffs thanks to Eric —but my head is spinning. The last thing I remember before everything goes black is Gabby saying, "Hold on Brandon. Help is coming. Stay with me! Help! Anyone?!"

Chapter Twenty-One
GABBY

I feel like this is all my fault. Tears are rolling down my cheeks as Brandon's sticky, warm blood coats my hands. Out of the corner of my eye, I see Alyssa running towards me. I keep telling Brandon to hold on and stay with me. I have no idea how badly he's inured, and all I can do is pray that there's no major damage.

"An ambulance is on the way," Alyssa says as she kneels down on the other side of Brandon.

I nod my head in acknowledgement as I continue to sob and talk to Brandon, not knowing if he can even hear me. A few minutes later I can hear more sirens approaching, and doors slamming as paramedics rush towards us.

The next moments are a blur as I'm pushed out of the way so they can work on Brandon. I'm vaguely aware of Eric saying something as he comes up beside Alyssa and I. All I can do is stand here and watch as Brandon is wheeled on a stretcher to the ambulance and lifted inside.

"Gabby?" Eric says as he gently touches my shoulder.

I shake my head to snap back to what's going on around me, and look at him with tear-filled eyes. "What?" I ask shakily.

"I said we should get you cleaned up," Eric says.

"No! I need to get to the hospital! Your best friend was just shot! How are you not worried?!"

"Alright, alright. Calm down. I *am* worried. I've just been trained to stay calm in these situations for work. Come on, I'll drive," he says. He motions for Alyssa who has been picking up Brandon's cooler and towel from where they lay scattered on the ground. The two of them lead me to his car and we quickly climb in to follow the ambulance to the emergency room.

Alyssa tries to comfort me as Eric drives us to the hospital, following the ambulance. "He's going to be alright, Gabby," Alyssa says. "And Tim is going away for a long, long time."

"How do you know?! I thought he was going away for a long time the last time!"

"True," Alyssa says calmly. "But this time he's

going away for attempted murder—and there were a lot of witnesses."

I take a deep breath and shake my head. I hope Alyssa's right about Tim being locked up for a long time. I also hope that it's just for *attempted* murder—I'm not sure what I'll do if Brandon actually dies.

We pull into the parking lot and I jump out of the car to sprint inside, barely waiting for Eric's car to stop moving. I run up to the front desk. "May I help you?" asks the nurse.

"My boyfriend Brandon Edwards was just brought in with a gunshot wound. How is he doing? Where is he?" I frantically ask.

"I'm sorry ma'am. If you're not family, I can't give you any information."

"But I'm his girlfriend!"

"I'm sorry ma'am. I still can't release any information to you."

Tears spill out of my eyes as I pace back and forth. I see Eric and Alyssa walk into the emergency room and I make my way towards them. "They won't give me any information because I'm not family."

"I know. I called Brandon's grandparents and they're on their way. In the meantime, let me see if I can find anything out, okay?"

"How? You're not related either," I ask in confusion.

"I'm law enforcement—besides, Brandon had me added as a medical contact for emergencies. We listed each other years ago in case anything happened to us and our families couldn't get here for some reason."

As Eric goes to try to find out what's happening with Brandon, Alyssa puts her arm around my shoulders and leads me to a chair to sit down. She sits in the chair next to me. "It's going to be alright, Gabby. I'm here for you—whatever you need."

"Thanks, Alyssa," I say shakily. "Right now, I just need you here with me. I don't know what I'm going to do if—"

"Stop right there. Don't think like that! He's going to be alright," Alyssa says reassuringly as I rest my head in my hands.

"Damn right he will be," says a familiar voice. I look up to see Brandon's grandfather standing next to me.

"I'm so sorry. It's all my fault," I say.

"Oh, nonsense!" says Brandon's grandmother as she pulls me into a hug. "Eric told us what happened. You had nothing to do with it dear. Don't blame yourself for something that you had no control over."

"But—maybe if I had just gone somewhere with Tim—lead him away—"

"Gabby. There's nothing you could have done.

Stop blaming yourself. Brandon wouldn't want you to feel responsible," she says.

Eric joins us where we're all sitting. "Hi, Mr. and Mrs. Edwards," he says before turning to look at me. "Alright. Brandon's in surgery to remove the bullet from his shoulder and repair some muscle damage. It didn't hit any vital organs and doctors expect him to make a full recovery."

"Really?" I ask, hopeful for the first time since this whole ordeal started.

"Yes, really," says Eric.

"Oh thank goodness."

Later, the surgeon walks through the doors and informs us all that surgery went as well as expected and Brandon is in recovery. I finally breathe a sigh of relief. "You can go in to see him now. He should be waking up from the anesthesia soon," the doctor says.

"You can go in, Gabby. We'll give you two a few minutes alone first," says Brandon's grandma.

"Are you sure?" I ask.

"Of course!" his grandpa answers. "We just needed to hear that he's alright. I think you need to see him the most."

"Thank you," I say as I stand to follow the doctor back to Brandon's room.

When I walk in, I see Brandon lying on the bed, hooked up to monitors and IVs with his arm in a sling. I can't help but choke back a sob, seeing him lying there so helplessly. I pull a chair up next to his bed and take his hand in mine before letting my tears fall once again. As I sit with my head hanging, sobbing next to Brandon's bed, I feel him reach up to wipe away a tear from my face. Slowly I lift my head to see Brandon's sleepy eyes looking up at me. "Hey," he says weakly.

"Hey," I say with a shaky voice. "I'm so sorry, Brandon."

"What happened?" he asks.

"You don't remember?"

"Not really. The last thing I remember is some angry man yelling at you."

"Brandon—he shot you."

He closes his eyes and says, "I remember now. Who was he?"

"That man, Tim, was my ex-boyfriend. The reason I moved to Wilkins Harbor was to hide from him. He fell in with the wrong crowd and that's when I planned to move here. I ended up moving early because one night I came home from work and overheard them planning a bank robbery. He threatened to kill me, and I ran," I say as I look away.

"Didn't you go to the police when he threatened you?" Brandon asks.

"Of course I did. I gave my statement about the threat and what I had heard. They arrested him, but I guess he got released early. I can't believe they let him out! I never thought he would find me here."

Brandon nods his head and swallows. "When I saw him pull that gun, Gabby—I've never been so scared in my life."

"He was aiming for me. Why did you push me out of the way?" I ask.

"Because Gabby—I love you! The thought of something happening to you wasn't something I could handle. I had to protect you, even if it meant putting myself in danger."

"You—you love me?" I ask with wide eyes.

"Yes. I love you. I love you more than anything, Gabby. I didn't think it was possible for me to love anyone ever again after Olivia—but then I met you. I tried to fight it, but I can't anymore. I love you."

Tears stream down my face as I lean down to kiss him. "I love you too, Brandon."

A few weeks later as Brandon and I are walking, hand in hand, along the shore of Lake Superior behind my house, I say, "I never thanked you by the way."

Brandon cocks his head to look at me and raises his eyebrow. "Thanked me? For what?"

"For saving my life that day. If you hadn't pushed me out of the way and taken the bullet for me, I'd probably be dead."

"I'd take a bullet for you any day," he says as he leans down to kiss me.

"Well, I want you to know, I'd do the same for you. My heart belongs to you now, Brandon."

"And mine belongs to you."

THE END

THANK YOU FOR READING!

If you enjoyed this story, please take a second to leave a review on Amazon. I appreciate your support.

Be sure to sign up for my newsletter at https://www.emorie-cole.com to get details about upcoming projects and access to exclusive content.

Keep reading for the link to preorder Book 2 of the Wilkins Harbor series, which follows Alyssa and Eric. Your favorite characters from Book 1 will also be making an appearance.

ALSO BY EMORIE COLE

Romance in the Keweenaw Collection

<u>Wilkins Harbor Series</u>

Accidental Love: Wilkins Harbor Book 2 (Preorder)

Midnight Carriage Kiss - Book 3 (Coming Soon)

<u>Standalones</u>

Unexpected Love on Christmas Eve: A Second Chance
Romance

ACKNOWLEDGEMENTS

I want to thank my wonderful husband for giving me the support to follow my dreams. Without him, my writing wouldn't be possible. He has been a huge help to me with advertising and website design. He has also been an amazing sounding board for ideas, a helping hand with editing, and isn't afraid to give me critique.

ABOUT THE AUTHOR

Emorie Cole is a small town girl who loves to show her creative side through her writing. She wants her readers to be swept into the world of steamy, small town romances where they'll feel emotional bonds being formed between new loves and second chances.

When she's not writing you can find her curled up with a good book, spending time with her family, playing with her dog, and enjoying the seasons in the beautiful Upper Peninsula of Michigan.

facebook.com/emoriecole

twitter.com/Emorie_Cole

instagram.com/emoriecole

Made in the USA
Monee, IL
28 March 2021